FORWARD

PASS

A PODIUM SPORTS ACADEMY BOOK

LORNA SCHULTZ
NICHOLSON

JAMES LORIMER & COMPANY LTD., PUBLISHERS
TORONTO

James Lorimer & Company Ltd., Publishers acknowledges the support of the Ontario Arts Council. We acknowledge the financial support of the Government of Canada through the Canada Book Fund for our publishing activities. We acknowledge the support of the Canada Council for the Arts which last year invested $24.3 million in writing and publishing throughout Canada. We acknowledge the Government of Ontario through the Ontario Media Development Corporation's Ontario Book Initiative.

Cover design: Meredith Bangay

Library and Archives Canada Cataloguing in Publication

Schultz Nicholson, Lorna
    Forward pass / Lorna Schultz Nicholson.

(A Podium Sports Academy book)
Issued also in an electronic format.
ISBN 978-1-4594-0373-4 (bound).—ISBN 978-1-4594-0372-7 (pbk.)

    I. Title. II. Series: Schultz Nicholson, Lorna Podium Sports Academy book.

PS8637.C58F67 2013   jC813'.6   C2012-907832-8

James Lorimer & Company Ltd.,
Publishers
317 Adelaide Street West, Suite 1002
Toronto, ON, Canada
M5V 1P9
www.lorimer.ca

Distributed in the United States by:
Orca Book Publishers
P.O. Box 468
Custer, WA USA
98240-0468

Printed and bound in Canada
Manufactured by Friesens Corporation in Altona, Manitoba, Canada in February 2013.
Job #82159

CHAPTER ONE

Bodies blocked my view. Rain drizzled from clouds that, in just ten minutes, had turned from cobalt blue to dark grey. Storm clouds in Calgary could roll in from the mountains in seconds, it seemed. And with the rain came the wind. I squinted to keep the ball in sight.

Don't lose it. Don't lose it.

I bounced on the balls of my feet, the ground beneath me becoming slippery. I shifted from side to side, trying to get the best view possible of the play in front of me. Water dripped down my face. Rule number one of soccer goalkeeping: always keep the ball in sight. I blinked to get the water out of my eyes. I scanned the players in front of me, all trying to get a foot on the ball. Rule number two of soccer goalkeeping: always anticipate the next move.

Out of the corner of my eye I saw my Edmonton Royals opponent on the goal crease line, and she had control of the ball, moving it deftly in her feet. Without losing sight of the ball, I quickly glanced to her side and saw the other attacker, in the open. Would the girl with the ball pass or shoot? I had to be ready for either. I knew my teammates were trying to kick the ball away, but they weren't succeeding. The girl drew her leg back, and by the angle and speed, I knew she was going to kick at the net. And it was going to be hard and high.

I saw her make contact. I sank into my crouch, then at exactly the right moment exploded up into the air. Using my arms to gain height, I stretched to the top of my net. My only chance was to block the shot, because it was too high to catch. I was almost at the height of my jump when fingers in front of me touched the ball.

The whistle blew. I groaned. My teammate and captain, Sophia, had flipped the ball off her fingers. The ref made the motion: hand ball.

Now we had a penalty, which meant the opposition had a penalty kick. I blew out a great gust of air and clapped my gloved hands together to get rid of the crud. Then I wiped my face with my sleeve. If only the rain would hold off coming down hard. Stopping a penalty shot in any weather wasn't easy. But the wet ground could hinder my dive.

Sophia looked at me and mouthed, "Sorry." She must have been trying to head it. I

I raised my hand in a gesture that told her it was okay, I could handle this. The score was 2–1. We were ahead and if I let this goal in, the game would be tied. I couldn't allow that.

"Time?" I asked Sophia. The game was close to being over and the refs were trying to get it finished before thunder sounded and lightning struck.

She gave me a quick nod and approached the ref. I watched the interaction, and within seconds she ran back to me. "Two minutes, and sorry again."

"It's okay," I replied, rubbing my hands on the sides of my legs. "She's a lefty. She'll go right."

Sophia patted me on the shoulder. "I have faith in you. Stay calm."

I nodded with complete confidence.

Calm. What a word. In this moment, calm was an illusion because my heart was ticking underneath my jersey, causing my entire body to vibrate. When Sophia rejoined our teammates, now positioned behind the goal kick line, I sucked in air, willing myself to focus. Even if my pounding heart made my body buzz, I had to look calm on the outside. It was so important when facing a penalty shot. My job was to put all the pressure on the penalty shooter.

The ref cleared the penalty zone. The lone shooter stood behind the ball, which was perfectly perched on the specific penalty-shot spot, eleven metres away from me. I stood tall and stared my shooter in the eye. Then . . .

I winked at her.

She blinked.

She walked toward the ball and moved it just a fraction. The ref rechecked the ball to make sure it was positioned properly. The corners of my mouth curled up ever so slightly. I had her. I'd made her nervous and she was going to kick to the right. I knew that by how she had changed the position of the ball. I moved slightly left, making her think that I thought she was going left. I saw her smile a little. She'd taken the bait. Now I was eighty percent sure she was going right.

The whistle blew. I stared at her plant foot and the ball. It was important to watch the plant foot because most often the ball went where the foot was pointing. And hers was pointing right. Now I was over ninety percent convinced.

She strode toward the ball. Just before she kicked it, I moved my upper body left, but held my stance with my lower body. My little fake to the left would give her the confidence to shoot right. Sure enough, she shot right.

As soon as she made contact, I dove to the right, stretching out my arms, using every inch of my body to make the catch. When I felt the ball in my arms, I hugged it tight. Then I crashed to the ground, landing on my hip with a thud. I slid in mud toward the goalpost. I heard cheers from the sidelines. I scrambled to stand and mud dripped down my legs. Immediately, I swung my leg back and kicked the ball down the field, sending my teammates running.

With both teams down the field, I was alone in my net, so I touched my hip. The padding in my shorts saved me from intense pain, although I would still have a bruise; nothing that ice couldn't fix.

The game ended with the score still 2–1. My teammates ran to me, giving me big congrats. Sophia hugged me and said, "I owe you one."

I laughed and replied, "One day you'll save my butt. And it will be in the biggest game of our lives."

"How about" — she grinned at me — "in Texas at the tournament when we play some of those top American high schools?" Her blond ponytail swung as she bobbed her head. She held up her hand and we high-fived. "I am so pumped for that tourney."

I looked up at the dark sky. "It'll be great to get out of this weather."

"Sun, heat. Totally awesome." She shut one eye to look at me. "You took a nasty dive."

"Ice. It's all about ice."

She nodded. I liked and respected Sophia as captain; she was always positive and kept our team focused. Not an easy job.

After shaking hands we all trudged off the field. On the sidelines we gathered in our post-game circle and stuck our hands in the middle.

"Three cheers for the Royals," said Sophia.

"Hip, hip, hooray. Hip, hip, hooray. Hip, hip, hooray."

Then Sophia yelled, "And three cheers for Podium!"

This time we shouted at the top of our lungs. "Hip, hip, hooray!"

Our head coach, Lori Swanson, or Coach Lori as we called her, joined our circle and said, "Great game, ladies. Great execution. I thought our defence was extremely strong. And, Parmita" — she looked right at me — "you read that penalty shot really well."

I held up my hand in thanks.

Without so much as a pause, Coach Lori continued, "I'm not going to keep you longer than I have to in this rain. Go on in and get dry."

As soon as Coach Lori walked away, the chatter began about which restaurant we would go to after showering. It was late Sunday afternoon and we often went somewhere to eat following an afternoon game.

Soaked to the skin, I gathered my belongings. I threw

my extra clothing into my bag, which had been put under a tarp to stay dry. A blistering hot shower was on my mind, big time. I swear I could taste the steam. I had just picked up my bag when one of our assistant coaches, Caroline Reilly, put her hand on my shoulder. Her touch sent shivers down my body.

"How's the hip?" she asked. "You landed pretty hard." She moved her hand from my shoulder to my hip, gently touching the padding on my shorts.

"A little bruised," I said. "I'll get ice." I shivered. "Thinking about ice is almost more than I can handle. All I want is a hot shower."

"You dove hard, girl. Ice it for at least ten before hitting the shower and then ice it again."

"Yeah," I said, "I know." Sometimes Caroline treated me like I was a novice. I'd been playing soccer since I was five and I've been a goalkeeper since I was ten. In Saskatchewan I'd played on a boys' team until I was fourteen because I was recruited by the coaches. Boys kicked hard, so I knew all about diving and icing. I moved a step away from Caroline, wanting her hand off my hip.

"Great read on the play, by the way." Her hand fell to her side. Her smoky grey eyes seemed to see right through me.

I yanked off my headband and ran my hand through my messed-up hair. It would need a bottle of conditioner lathered into it before I could run a comb through it. I'd inherited a head of thick black hair from my East Indian father, and it was a tangled mess after every game. My mother had fine straight sandy-blond hair, which would have been much easier to deal with as a soccer goalkeeper, especially when it rained.

Caroline reached out and touched my cheek with her finger. "You're covered in mud."

"Yeah," I said. To be covered in mud as a goalie was a good thing, for it meant I had done my job. Caroline always noticed how hard I worked and I appreciated that. Our team's backup goalie, Jessie White, approached us, and Caroline quickly pulled away her hand.

I flushed with embarrassment, so I ducked my head and swiped my face with my sleeve.

"You held your ground and made her play to you," Caroline said in a businesslike tone. "That was smart and strategic."

"You did such a good job, Parm," said Jessie. "I wish I had half your focus."

Caroline nodded at Jessie's comment, but she didn't touch her like she touched me. "Your turn will come," she said to her. "We have to keep practicing."

Jessie nodded. In grade eleven and in her first year at Podium Sports Academy, Jessie still had a lot to learn. Caroline, however, was patient with both of us and she worked at our individual levels, which I liked. And she never treated Jessie as only a backup goalkeeper.

Caroline was a native of Calgary and seven years older than I was. A former Canadian National Team goalie, she had retired because of a knee injury and now ran camps and clinics all over the country for younger kids. Podium had jumped at the chance to hire her as a part-time goalkeeping coach, and she worked exclusively with Jessie and me. When I'd heard the news she was coming to our school, I'd been excited. I wanted to play on the National Team and be in the Olympics. She could be my "in" because she knew the coaches and what they liked.

"Your turn will totally come," I said to Jessie.

"That's the plan," said Jessie.

Suddenly I felt chilled. I started walking toward the school, hoping we could continue our conversation on the way.

"Next week," said Caroline, falling into step with me, "I want to work on catching high balls. Both of you have decent height and a good vertical, but I want to help you get even more height."

"Sounds good." I was five foot ten, which for a goalie was decent.

Caroline turned to Jessie and said, "I'd like to work on some other things with you too."

As they chatted in detail about drills Caroline would do with Jessie, I glanced across the field and saw my friend Allie. She was almost six foot one and Podium's top-scoring basketball player. She was standing under a red umbrella with a few other friends, and I thought, she *would* bring a red umbrella. A smile spread across my face as I watched her laughing and twirling the thing.

I scanned the group to see who had tagged along with her: Jax, Kade, and Carrie. Carrie? Why was Carrie here? Something bristled inside me. I didn't want Allie hanging out with Carrie. They did girly things together like shop and go for breakfast at Starbucks and wear makeup, and to me that was not Allie. That was her trying to be someone else.

I was glad to see that Nathan wasn't with the group. If he had been, it might mean Allie and Nathan were getting back together, and he wasn't good for her either. A lacrosse player with a mop of long hair, Nathan was too irresponsible for me and I didn't think he treated Allie right. Allie had recently spent hours confiding in me about him; I'd sat on her bed and listened and hugged her when she cried.

To see her with Carrie again caused a stabbing pain in my heart, a pain worse than the one on my hip. Was Allie confiding in Carrie again? Was she sharing everything with her that she'd shared with me?

Allie must have felt my gaze because she waved. Then she cupped her hand around her mouth and yelled across the field, "Great game, Parm!"

I held up my thumb.

Caroline turned from Jessie and gave me an odd look. "You guys are pretty tight, eh?"

"Yeah. She's my bff."

"How's her knee? I heard she's injured."

"She's wearing a brace and she's sidelined for a few more days. It's killing her not to play."

"Are you heading to the restaurant for the post-game meal?" Caroline asked. "I was thinking of going and we could continue our conversation about things we should be working on." She turned back to Jessie. "You too, Jess."

Coaches weren't supposed to fraternize with the players after games because at Podium Sports Academy, they were hired and paid to coach. They were like teachers. It was a no-nonsense school that treated athletes like professionals and expected the same from their coaches. Maybe she just wanted to make sure I would go since she was always harping about how important it was for everyone to be part of the team and act like a team.

"I'm in for sure," said Jessie. She never missed a social opportunity.

Caroline slid a glance at me. "So . . . what about you?"

I shrugged. I often begged off, but only because of time. My short-term goal was to attend the University of Toronto and play on their soccer team while getting my undergrad in science. During that time, I also wanted to make the National Team and hopefully, when the time came, be on the Olympic Team. My long-term goal was to go to Harvard Medical School and ultimately become a surgeon. All my goals meant I needed high nineties in every subject. And that meant I had to log big hours studying.

I glanced in Allie's direction again. Maybe I could hook up with her after I ate with my team, even for just an hour or so.

"I got most of my homework done last night," I replied to Caroline. "So, yeah, I'll go."

"Good," said Caroline. She furrowed her eyebrows and said, "It will be a team deal though. I don't think your . . . bff should tag along with us."

CHAPTER TWO

When we reached Allie and her gang, I said to Caroline and Jessie, "I'll catch up to you guys in a minute."

Caroline didn't break stride and ignored my friends as she walked by them.

"Hey, Parm, great job," said Allie. "Good going on the penalty shot."

"Thanks," I replied.

"Yeah," said Jax. "You really dove." He mimicked my movement and grimaced. "Ouch. You must get a lot of bruises."

His antics made me laugh. Since I'd met Allie, I'd laughed more and socialized more than I ever had in my life. I was an only child and my life in Saskatoon had been quiet. All I did was play soccer and study. "*You're* the snowboarder," I said to Jax. "*You* must get the bruises."

Carrie hip-checked Jax. "Yeah, Jaxie. How does it feel to crash on packed snow after doing a flip thirty feet in the air? Now that's a big ouch."

"Her dive was still really impressive," said Jax.

"So, Parm," Allie said to me, "what are you up to now?"

She wiggled one eyebrow up and down, her signature expression. "Besides having a shower?"

Everyone laughed at my mud-covered face and body.

"Ice, shower, food," I said. "In that order." Remembering Caroline's words, I added, "I have to eat with my team. But I could hook up with you after."

Allie glanced at Carrie. "You still want to go for wings somewhere?"

"Sure." Carrie always did this head-bob thing when she talked. The move annoyed me because it didn't suit her fierce-competitor personality.

Carrie smiled at the boys. "Anyone else in?"

"Duh," replied Kade. "I'm always up for wings."

"Me too," said Jax.

"You're on, girlfriend." Allie held up her hand and Carrie slapped it back, and I wanted to turn away, but I faked a smile and watched the interaction. Sometimes I felt like an intruder with this group of athletes. I'd never belonged to a big group of friends. Having one good friend was enough for me. This group thing, which Allie liked, was a challenge, but because she wanted me to be involved, I was putting my best foot forward.

I quickly turned to Allie. "So did you want to hook up later?"

"Text me," she said.

Most of my teammates were already showering or finished when I entered the change room. Sophia was towelling her hair, and when she saw me, she burst out laughing. "Go look at yourself in the mirror."

Another teammate, Louise — we all called her Loo-Loo — jumped up on the bench, dressed only in her bra and underwear. "Three cheers for Parmita!"

I put up my hands to stop the cheering. "Who's got the ice packs?"

Loo-Loo jumped off the bench and tossed an ice pack to me, and I caught it in one hand. After pulling off my soccer shorts, I sat on the bench and placed the ice on my hip bone. I leaned against the wall, knowing there was nothing else to do for ten minutes but sit. The room was filled with the after-game buzz of hair dryers, laughter, and chit-chat, as my teammates applied makeup and got dressed. The ice numbed my hip and took away the pain. It would return soon enough, but for now I was happy the sting was gone. After the ten minutes were up, I figured I'd better get in the shower, otherwise I'd be late for the team meal.

I undressed, grabbed my towel off the hook, and wrapped it around my body.

"See you there," said Sophia, tossing her long silky blond hair. Everyone knew she was National Team material, and because she always dressed in the latest styles and looked amazing, she'd also be great advertising material. One day, if she continued playing and made the National Team, her face with its peaches and cream complexion would be on a cereal box, not the face of some female hockey player. Plus, of all my teammates, she was the one I could confide in the most.

I held up my hand. "Yeah, give me five and I'll be showered and dressed."

I was on my way to the shower area when Caroline

barged in the change room. "How's the hip?" she asked me.

"It's been iced."

"Good. See you at the restaurant?" Her question almost came out as a demand.

I frowned. "Yeah, I said I'd go."

"Do you need a ride?"

"I have a car," I replied. She knew I drove to school every day. Why did she ask me if I needed a ride?

"Just making sure," she said. Then she yelled, "Anyone need a ride?"

"I do!" Jessie yelled back.

After she left with Jessie in tow, Sophia whispered to me, "How do you like her as your goalie coach?"

I shrugged. "She knows her stuff."

"She shouldn't offer to drive athletes like that," she said.

"Maybe she's just being nice." I turned and headed to the shower.

The hot water felt amazing, and I stood under the shower for a long time, so long that everyone was gone by the time I finished. Alone in the change room, I pulled out my phone. No text from Allie. I threw the phone back in my bag, towelled my hair, and got dressed. I tried to run a comb through my tangled hair, but even though I'd used loads of conditioner, it was no use. I combed it with my fingers and left the change room.

I arrived at the restaurant and steered my little Subaru hatchback into the last available parking spot. Upon entering the restaurant, I could hear the girls before I saw them. This team was the craziest, loudest team I had ever played on and by far the most skilled. When I approached the table, I noticed the last empty seat was beside Caroline. As soon as she saw me, she stood and pulled out the chair.

"I saved you a seat, Parm," she said.

"Thanks." I sat down and picked up a menu. "You guys order yet?"

"Everyone else did," Caroline replied, "but I waited for you."

"You didn't have to do that." I scanned the menu. She leaned over so our shoulders were touching and pointed to the pizza section. My breath quickened and I fidgeted in my seat. Why did she have to sit so close to me?

"They have great pizzas here," she said. "They're cooked in a wood oven." Her breath felt warm on my face.

When I saw chicken Caesar salad, I closed the menu and leaned away from her.

"What are you having, Parm?" Hazel asked from across the table. A defender on the team, Hazel wore her blond hair in a short spiky cut and was built like a truck. She was only five-six, but she had thick-muscled legs and one heck of a boot. Not many strikers got by her. I loved having her play in front of me.

"Chicken Caesar. You?"

"Chicken wings and garlic toast." She smiled at me, her blue eyes dancing and her round cherub face lighting up the room. Hazel was one of those always-happy people.

The mention of chicken wings made me pull out my phone and check my texts. Nothing.

"Heck of a game today," Hazel said.

I put my phone on the table and glanced over at her again. "Thanks. You too. You saved my butt a few times."

"Texas is going to be awesome. I can't wait!"

"There'll be some good teams," piped up Caroline. "I've played in that tournament before."

Caroline and Hazel chatted for a few moments while I fired off a text to Allie telling her I was still at the restaurant. I held my phone in my hand waiting for a reply, since Allie usually responded right away. Ten minutes passed and no buzz.

Our meals arrived and I put my phone back down and dug into my salad. I was anxious to finish so I could either hook up with Allie or get back to my billets' to read through my chemistry notes. Maybe Allie could come over too. We had worked really hard on a chemistry experiment together, and now that it was over, she didn't come by as much.

My billets would be at church; they went twice every Sunday.

Within an hour, everyone was finished eating and standing up to leave. I followed the pack, tugging on my jean jacket. I shoved my phone into the top pocket. It buzzed. I yanked it out. Yes. Allie.

"You're really hooked to your phone," said Caroline.

I ignored her as I read the text, immediately disappointed because Allie said she was heading home. She was tired but would see me at school in the a.m. As I was walking out, I felt a hand on my shoulder. I turned to see Caroline. My first reaction was to look around the restaurant to see if anyone noticed her touching me.

"See you tomorrow," she said. "I've got some great drills for you to try."

"Sure," I said as I moved a small step away from her. I lifted my hand, gave her a little wave, and immediately hightailed it to my car. When I climbed in, I sat there for a minute before backing out. I was breathing as if I had just done a wind sprint.

When I got to my billets' house, located in the northwest community of Brentwood, I was surprised to see their car in the driveway. I entered the house through the side door and heard the murmur of their voices in the kitchen. At first I had found living with another family difficult, but as time passed it became easier. I felt lucky that my family was kind and the mom was an amazing cook.

The house wasn't big but it was comfortable. I climbed the six stairs to the kitchen. My room was downstairs and my access was on the other side of the kitchen. The Reimer family sat at the kitchen table with their Bibles open.

"Hi," I said quietly, not wanting to disturb what looked like Bible study. "I hope I'm not interrupting."

Mrs. Reimer closed her Bible, scraped her chair back, and smiled at me. "Not at all. Perfect timing. We just finished reading a passage from the book of Mark."

"You didn't go to church tonight?" I hung my keys on the wooden key rack on the wall.

Ten-year-old Thomas sniffled. "I'm not feeling very good. I think I got a cold watching your game. We had to leave right away because I was sneezing." He wiped his nose with his sleeve before he said, "You made such a good save on the penalty shot." When he looked at me, his eyes lit up and I had this funny feeling he might be faking his cold.

Ruth, who had just turned twelve a week ago and looked like a modern-day Orphan Annie with her crazy red hair and fair skin, rolled her pale eyes, at me as if to say she knew her brother wasn't sick either. She glanced at the kitchen clock and clapped her hands. "I got *Glee* taped! Watch it with me, Parm. I don't have to go to bed for an hour." She jumped up and I noticed she was wearing her new skin-tight jeans. She'd shown them to me yesterday.

It was only eight o'clock. If I got two good hours of studying in, I could probably get in the high nineties or even a hundred. As an only child, I enjoyed the company of the Reimer kids, who had become like a little brother and sister to me. "Sure," I said.

"Parmita, are you hungry?" Mrs. Reimer asked.

"I'm good, thanks. I ate with the team."

"I could make you girls some popcorn?"

"Sure," I replied. Ruth skipped to the family room and I followed. When we were out of earshot, Ruth whispered, "I taped *Gossip Girl* too. Don't tell my dad."

I ruffled her hair. "That one I won't watch with you. I don't want to get you in trouble."

She jutted out her bottom lip. "Aww."

I gently pushed her to the sofa. "Let's get *Glee* on, girl. I've got homework."

"You've always got homework."

"That's because I want good marks."

She tossed her head. "I don't care about school marks because I want to be an actor and do a kissing scene with someone like Justin Bieber." She put her hands to her mouth and squealed.

I glanced back to the kitchen, hoping Mrs. Reimer wasn't coming in with the popcorn yet. If she heard Ruth talking like that, she would probably scold her. Ruth was proving to be a bit of a challenge for her parents because their strict religious views were in direct conflict with Ruth's craving for pop culture. Within seconds Ruth had *Glee* playing on the television and I settled in to watch, even though it wasn't my type of show. I liked watching medical shows like *Grey's Anatomy* on TV.

Partway through, my phone rang. I quickly checked it, and when I saw it was Allie, I jumped up.

"Where are you going?" Ruth asked. "This is, like, the best part. They're singing."

I held up my finger. "Gimme a second." Then I pressed the phone to my ear. "Hey," I said.

"Okay, so this is so exciting!" Allie rushed her words. "You know Donald, from the track and field team? He's a sprinter."

"Uh, yeah, I think so." I didn't know that many of the athletes. Allie was my first real friend and I'd met everyone from her circle.

"He phoned and wants me to go to a Halloween party with him! And he's six foot three — taller than me!" She squealed her words almost like Ruth had when she'd mentioned Justin Bieber.

Something caught in my throat. "Great," I answered with as much enthusiasm as I could muster.

Allie obviously didn't notice my lack of excitement because she continued. "And here's my plan. You should go with his friend Gary. The four of us could go together."

"Gary?"

"Yeah. He's a diver. And hot."

"I don't have a costume," I muttered.

"We'll get them together. We can go shopping. Hey, maybe we can be the Three Stooges."

"Three Stooges? There's just two of us."

"Carrie's in too. She's going with Jax. Oh my gawd, she could be Curly." Allie started laughing.

Suddenly her phone gave off some little beeps. "That's my other line."

I could tell she had pulled her phone away from her face because the line went silent for a few seconds. When she came back on, she said, "It's Carrie. I gotta go. I have to tell her. She'll be so jacked."

I fell back against the sofa and tossed some popcorn in my mouth. Without taking her gaze off the television, Ruth asked, "Was that Allie?"

"Yeah. She wants me to go to a Halloween party."

Ruth pouted and crossed her arms. "My parents won't let me go out for Halloween. They say I can't because we're Christians. I think it's a dumb rule."

"It's not that much fun, trust me," I said.

CHAPTER THREE

"Two more!" yelled Caroline.

I jumped from side to side: crouching, exploding, crouching, exploding. My legs screamed in pain. Jessie grunted beside me, swinging her arms to get higher. One thing about Jessie; she was a hard worker. Sure, I pushed her but she pushed me too. Just looking at her made me swing my arms to get more height.

"Good," said Caroline when we'd finished. "Take a water break."

I shook out my legs as I sucked water from my bottle. Sweat dripped off my forehead and I wiped it with my sleeve. The rest of the team was down the field running lines. We had all warmed up together, but then we had split off. They ran lines while Jessie and I worked on vertical jumps, lateral moves, and quick feet drills.

A couple of minutes later Caroline said, "One more set." She was sure putting us through our paces.

Jessie moaned.

"We can do it, girl," I encouraged her.

Jessie exhaled loudly, blowing loose strands of hair off

her face. But she nodded once and said, "Okay. I'm ready.

We both crouched low. Before even jumping my legs hurt. I sucked in a deep breath and waited. When Caroline yelled "Go!" Jessie and I jumped back and forth, springing as high as we could before landing. We locked gazes to keep motivated.

After ten each side I put my hands on my knees and leaned over to catch my breath. Jessie collapsed on the ground. I glanced at her. "You'll seize up if you lie there," I gasped. I could hardly get the words out.

"When you're ready," Caroline said, "I want you guys in the net for some ball drills." I was still leaning over, trying to breathe, when she passed behind me and slapped me on the butt.

Twenty minutes later and too many catches to count, we were reunited with the rest of the team. Coach Lori ran the remainder of the practice, and Jessie and I took turns in the net, stopping shots as Lori ran several passing and forward-versus-defence drills. Caroline stood off to the side and gave Jessie and me tips.

At the end of practice Coach Lori called us in. "Great practice," she said. I liked Lori. She was a no-nonsense coach, which was my style. She didn't play favourites and ran a well-organized, disciplined practice. Playing on boys' teams, I'd had a couple of coaches who couldn't control disruptive behaviours.

"I'd like to have a meeting tomorrow after practice about Texas," Lori went on. "There are a few things I'd like to go over." She looked at Caroline. "And I'd like you to spend some time working on the goal kicks with Jessie and Parmita."

"For sure," said Caroline.

"See everyone tomorrow," said Coach Lori.

The team dispersed and I picked up my bag and slung it over my shoulder. Caroline approached me. "Can you be here twenty minutes before practice tomorrow?"

"Absolutely," I said. I had spare last block.

After showering, I texted Allie about Halloween costume shopping, and she sent a message back right away that her knee hurt too much. She sounded really bummed out. As I walked to my car, I decided I would take a detour and pop by her place.

Her billet mother opened the door dressed in what looked to be a really expensive suit. Allie lived with a young professional married couple — John Simpson and Abigail Reid. They had no children and the house was always spotless, unlike the Reimers', where backpacks cluttered the mud room and school papers were stuck with magnets to the refrigerator.

"Hi, Parmita," said Abigail. "Come on in. Allie's in her room." I slipped out of my shoes and Abigail bent over and lined them up. "Just so you know," she said to me, "she's very upset about her knee."

I walked through the living room with its glass tables and Persian rugs and padded down the hall to Allie's bedroom. For a second I stood outside the door. Then I knocked.

"Yeah?"

"Hey, it's me."

"Come on in, Parm."

I walked in to see Allie sprawled on her bed with an ice pack on her knee. I sat on the foot of the bed. "What happened?"

"I don't know," she groaned. "I thought it was getting better, then today at practice I did a jumpshot and it started to hurt again. It's not too too bad, but I'm worried."

"What about your MRI? Did it show anything?"

She shook her head and looked away. "I didn't have one and I don't need one," she muttered. Then she forced out a smile. "Anyway, it's not swollen anymore."

I reached over to lift the ice pack from her knee for a look, but she touched my hand to stop me. Her skin against mine felt velvety and soft.

"Don't," she said, gently moving my hand away. "It's okay. The X-ray showed nothing and I had an ultrasound done too. I think it's just me imagining things. I'm gonna play Saturday night."

"Okay." I gazed into her dark eyes and could see her pain and frustration. I just wanted to reach inside her and take it all away.

"The knee will get better," she said. "It has to. We've got a big tournament at Christmas. And I've got next year at Duke. I want to go to Duke so badly. It's all I've ever wanted." She put her head in her hands.

I placed my hand on her shoulder. "It will be okay by then, Allie. You just need to rest it. Maybe we shouldn't go out for Halloween. I'd stay in with you."

Immediately she looked up, her eyes glistening. "I'm going out for Halloween and that's final. I'll wear my brace. Donald is such a sweetie, Parm. I think I really like him. He's so different from Nathan."

My hand fell from her shoulder and I placed it in my lap. "You're not thinking of getting close to Donald already, are you? It hasn't been long since your breakup with Nathan."

"I know, I know." She looked upwards, then sighed loudly. But when she looked at me, there was definite excitement in her eyes. "But . . . it's so crazy. When I'm with him, I just want him to touch me. Nathan was like this comfortable blanket and Donald is electrical."

I looked down and started picking at the little pieces of lint on her comforter. "Wow," I said.

"It is like *wow*. Parm, it's nuts."

I slowly lifted my head and attempted to smile. "I'm happy for you."

"You are such a friend." She wiggled one eyebrow up and down. "You'll love Gary. He's so much fun."

I stood to leave. "I gotta go. I've got homework."

"Okay, Little Miss Surgeon. Thanks for stopping by."

Right on time the next afternoon, I walked across the field for my goal-kick practice. The brilliant sun shone high in an azure sky, and the air had the perfect tinge of fall crispness. All day everyone had been talking about what a beautiful day it was, and I should have been happy, but I wasn't. I kicked stones as I walked. I finally had a friend and now she had *another* boyfriend. Donald wasn't right for Allie either. I'd watched him flirting with Carrie at lunch. Allie was going to get hurt.

You can be there for her when that happens.

With that thought in mind, I started to jog across the field. I looked up at the perfect Alberta blue sky. Would it snow for Halloween? Snow in Saskatoon in October was normal. One Halloween I wore snow boots and a heavy winter jacket over my costume. I'd stopped going out in grade six because by then I was five foot six. But this year I *was* going out. Why?

To please Allie.

Caroline was waiting for me. No Jessie though.

"Where's Jessie?" I asked.

"She couldn't make it," said Caroline. "She has a test last period. I'll work with her after the meeting."

"Okay," I said. "Let me warm up first."

I ran around the field a few times, shifting side to side and running backwards. Caroline waited for me at the goalposts with a bag of balls.

When I finished warming up, I stood in the middle of the net and she went out on the field. Ball after ball I kicked out to her, trying to get as close as possible to where she was standing. Today was all about accuracy.

The time flew and soon the rest of the team joined us on the field.

"You're welcome to join Jessie and me after the meeting," Caroline said, holding a ball under her arm.

"I'd love to but I can't," I replied.

She dropped the ball and started playing with it in her feet. I could see how talented she was. "You know," she said, "I think you've got a solid chance of making the National Team." I continued to watch her feet move. I would have to get as good as she was. She had been the National Team goalie for six years, since she was eighteen. She looked up and winked at me before looking down at the ball again. "You keep working the way you are, and I'll put a call in for you just to let them know your skill and work ethic.

And, believe me, I wouldn't do that if I didn't think you were good enough."

"Wow," I said. "I'd really appreciate that." If she could do that for me, I'd be so grateful. Success often depended on good connections. My lawyer parents had drilled that into me.

She flipped the ball backwards with her foot, caught it, and stared at me. "We could go for coffee tonight to talk."

I didn't want to be seen in a coffee shop with my coach. "I, um, have a ton of homework."

"What about Friday?" Caroline persisted.

"I'm going out for Halloween."

Caroline rolled her eyes. "I hate dressing up. Are you, like, going to a party?" She dropped the ball to the ground again and started playing with it. Back and forth.

"Yeah. I'm going with a guy from the diving team."

She immediately stopped moving and looked at me with a puzzled expression on her face. "A guy?"

Why had I told her anything about my personal life? "Yeah," I replied, then turned and walked toward my teammates to get ready for practice.

The Texas meeting was short and sweet because Coach Lori ran it. I would be rooming with Loo-Loo and Hazel.

I left the meeting and called Allie.

"I got our costumes," she said. She sounded much more upbeat.

"Great." I tried to sound enthusiastic. "How was your practice today?"

"Coach wants me to rest. I'll be back next week. But

I don't want to talk about that. Where should we get dressed?"

"We can't at my billets'," I said. "They don't believe in Halloween."

"What? That's crazy. They have kids."

"Yeah, but they're okay," I said. "Each to their own."

"My place is kind of out too. I might make a mess. We'll go to Carrie's."

"Carrie's?"

"Yeah. Mr. and Mrs. Sandford are a hoot."

I didn't want to go to *Carrie's.*

CHAPTER FOUR

On Halloween night I drove over to Carrie's and sat in my car for a few moments before I got the nerve to get out. The streetlights shone brightly and most houses in the neighbourhood were lit up. Many were decorated with little tissue ghosts hanging from trees, RIP signs on the front lawns, cheap gaudy blow-up crap, and pumpkins, lots of glowing pumpkins.

The front lights of Carrie's billet house were on, and carved pumpkins lined the stairs. Her billets were an older couple and they still celebrated. My parents still celebrated too; my mother loved Halloween. Tonight the Reimers had made a big deal of turning off all their lights. To them it was a pagan holiday.

Judging from the cars lined up in front of the Sandfords', I figured the guys were here already. I groaned. Why did I agree to this?

I knocked on the door and Carrie answered, ushering me in. "We're in the kitchen." Bowls of candy and little bags of chips sat in the front entranceway.

"You're not in your costume yet," I said.

She did a little dance with her shoulders. "We were waiting for you." Carrie had two personalities: girly-girl and fierce competitor. I liked her best as fierce competitor and I had to admit, I did think the flips and moves she did underwater were incredible.

I followed Carrie into the kitchen, and Allie, as soon as she saw me, put her arm around me, which made me relax a little. "Parm, you know everyone, right?"

I nodded. "Hi guys." I lifted my hand in a little wave. Donald and Jax said hello, but Gary gave me a finger-peace hello, which I acknowledged with a nod.

Did he think this was a date?

A quick glance around told me no one was drinking, and I was happy about that. I had never touched a drink in my life.

"So." Allie clapped her hands. "Let's get this party started." She threw me a black wig that looked like a mop and a big long lab coat. "You're Moe."

I put on the wig and everyone laughed. When I glanced at myself in the mirror, I also laughed. It did look hilarious. Next, the boys dressed as Charlie's Angels, and I had to grab my sides I was laughing so hard. Maybe the night would be more fun than I thought. Allie could do this to me — make me happy.

As we put on some crazy makeup to make the costumes that much better, little kids knocked on the door. Mr. and Mrs. Sandford took photos of us and we made goofy faces.

An hour later we got into Gary's SUV (even though I really wanted to take my own car). Carrie and Jax hopped into the back seat and Allie and Donald sat in the middle seat. That left me to sit in the front seat beside Gary. I got in and sat as close to the door as I could.

The party was in full swing when we arrived and the costumes ranged from Batman to Superman to devils and witches and monsters and nurses and, of course, sexy celebrities. As soon as I walked in, I saw Loo-Loo and Hazel. I think Loo-Loo was supposed to be Shrek and Hazel the donkey. Whatever they were, they looked ridiculous and hadn't gone to any great lengths to have the best costumes.

"Hey, Parm!" they yelled.

"I'll be back in a sec," I said to Gary.

I breathed a sigh of relief when I walked away from him. He was clinging to me like a bad rash.

"Your costume is so great," said Loo-Loo. "You guys actually *look* like the Three Stooges."

Loo-loo spun around, sending her donkey tail flying. "This is as good as ours get."

"I had help," I said.

Hazel leaned over and whispered, "You here with Gary?"

"Not really," I replied.

We chatted for a few more minutes until someone bumped into me from behind. I turned to see Nathan dressed as Zorro, wearing a mask and black cape.

"Sorry, Parm," he said.

"No biggie," I said.

"How's Allie doing?"

"She's still wearing her brace and fretting about her scholarship."

"Really? I talked to her yesterday and she said everything was okay."

"She's a good liar."

He shook his head and exhaled. "I still think about her all the time." He placed his hand on my shoulder. "She's lucky to have a friend like you."

I nodded. We had nothing more to say to each other so he turned and made his way to the kitchen, leaving me standing alone in the middle of a party. I scanned the room looking for Allie and finally spotted her, hanging on to Donald.

Suddenly, a hand snaked its way around my waist. I jumped in surprise.

"Having fun?" Gary whispered in my ear.

His hot breath almost made me gag. I ducked and tried to pull away from his grasp. "Yeah," I said.

He drew me closer to him again. Sweat beaded on my face and my stomach heaved. "Music's on," he whispered in my ear. "You wanna dance?"

I spun around to face him so I couldn't feel his breath on my ear and neck.

From across the room, I could see Allie smiling at me, giving me the okay sign. Did she think I liked Gary? My heart thudded to my toes and my shoulders sagged.

I forced a smile. "I have to, uh, hit the bathroom," I said. "Maybe in a bit."

A small bathroom was located at the front of the house by the entrance. I weaved through the bodies, but instead of going to the bathroom, which had a lineup, I headed outside. The crisp air smacked me in the face as I strode down the street toward the C-Train station. I whipped off my wig and used the lab coat to wipe the makeup off my face.

CHAPTER FIVE

"How was Halloween?" Ruth asked the next morning at breakfast. Mrs. Reimer had made pancakes and sausages.

"Ruthie," said her father. "Let's not talk about Halloween."

Yeah, let's not, I thought. I took the plate of pancakes and plopped just one on my plate.

"You need more than one pancake," said Mrs. Reimer to me.

I stared down at my plate and the thought of eating made me feel sick. Allie had texted me last night after I left the party and was so mad at me for leaving. I had tossed and turned all night. I didn't want her mad at me.

I glanced over at Ruth, and her face was contorted into an exaggerated pout. When Ruth's father lowered his head to read his Saturday morning newspaper, she stuck out her tongue at him. I hid my smile; at least Ruth could cheer me up.

"Um, pass the bacon," I said to her. Luckily Thomas was too busy feeding the dog the fat off his bacon to notice Ruth's gesture. He loved to tattle on her.

Still pouting, Ruth passed the bacon to me and I smiled

at her, took a piece, and placed it on my plate. Then I winked at her. The corner of her mouth lifted and suddenly both of us were smiling at our secret.

I took a bite of my pancake. Everything would be okay. I would tell Allie that I'd left because I wasn't feeling well.

Partway through breakfast I said to Mrs. Reimer, "I'm going away next weekend. I thought I should remind you."

"Oh, right. You're off to Dallas."

"Do you have to go?" Ruth whined. "This house is *way more fun* when you're here."

"I'll bring you and Thomas something back," I said. This time I winked at both her and Thomas.

"Yay!" Thomas threw his hands in the air.

After breakfast I went downstairs to my room. The Saturdays when we didn't have a game or practice were usually study days for me and they didn't happen often. Sometimes I went to the library if Ruth and Thomas were going to be home all day — Ruth loved coming to my room and sitting on my bed, which didn't help me study. But if the house was going to be quiet, I just worked in my room. Today the Reimer family had a church function, some all-day thing, so I decided to hole up in my room.

Two hours into reviewing all my notes from the previous week, my cell phone buzzed. I saw my home number and immediately answered it.

"Hey Mom," I said.

"How *are* you?" My mom spoke with such earnestness! "I haven't talked to you since Wednesday. I miss hearing your voice. I miss you, period."

"Yeah, me too. I'm good. Just doing some studying."

"Parmita, you study too much. You need to get out."

Here we go again. My mom always harped on me for studying too much and not socializing. She was always fretting that I didn't have enough friends and had never had a boyfriend or even been on a date. I sighed. Deep in my heart, I knew the boy-girl dating thing was not for me. After last night I had no desire to ever go on a date with a guy again. The trick would be when to come out to my parents and the rest of the world, but I had a plan: Christmas next year when I was in my first year of university. The thought of telling them their only child was a lesbian made me sick and nervous and clammy and . . . sad. They would be so disappointed in me. My father's East Indian family might disown me.

I scraped my desk chair back, stretched, then flopped on my bed. I needed a break. "You'll be happy to hear," I said, "that I got dressed up and went to a Halloween party last night and I'm going to a basketball game tonight."

"Oh, that's exciting! Okay, let's start with last night. Did you wear a costume? Where was the party? Who did you go with?"

My mom was, seriously, the land of fifty questions. Sometimes one text was five questions long. "Allie, Donald, Carrie, Jax, and a guy named Gary. He's a diver."

There was a little pause before she asked, "Were you on a date?"

Why did I tell her anything? She always tried to read more than there was into every conversation. Her excitement made me rub my forehead. I could feel a headache coming on. "Not really," I answered. "It just so happened that there were six of us."

"Oh." Her voice dropped and I could tell she was disappointed. But she quickly asked, "Was he nice, though? Could he be a potential date?"

"Mom, we just went to a party where there were tons of people. And, yes, I got dressed up in a costume."

"What did you wear?"

I knew mentioning the costume would throw her off the date topic. "Carrie, Allie, and I were the Three Stooges."

"How fun! I'm so happy that you're getting out with some of these athletes. Dad and I knew this school would be good for you. That you'd be with kindred spirits and perhaps come out of your shell. Is your friend Allie playing tonight?"

"Yeah." I didn't want to talk about Allie; she had been so mad at me last night for leaving the party. "How *is* Dad?" I changed the subject.

"He's got a big case this week so he's immersed in papers." She paused, then sighed. "I guess the apple doesn't far fall from the tree."

Both my parents were lawyers. My dad was a prosecutor and my mother an estate and family court lawyer. He took the work way more seriously than she did, or at least that's how it seemed to me. When I was little, she was the one who left the office early to pick me up from school and drive me to soccer. All my life I'd wanted to be like my dad and be the one who brought home stacks of files and worked until after midnight.

I laughed at her comment. "But that's a good thing, right?"

"Yes," she said, "it's a good thing. Although I'm glad you took some time to go out last night. Maybe this Gary could be your grad date."

"Grad is like months away! Stop planning."

"I guess I am getting a bit ahead of myself," she said. "Dad said he'd call you later tonight when he takes a break."

"'kay," I replied. "Well, I gotta go."

I tossed my phone on my bed and stared at the ceiling for a few minutes. *Grad date? Was she kidding me?* Just because she'd worn the long dress and done her hair in some crazy up-do, as she called it, didn't mean I had to. I loved my mom but, man, were we different. In baby pictures, I was dolled up in little dresses and those shiny black patent leather shoes. At around age six, when I started school, things changed when I refused to wear frills. I had even gone so far as to cut up all the pink dresses in my closet with scissors, telling her I would never wear frills again. Now, I didn't mind a skirt, but it had to be straight and with a jacket. Even at my grade eight graduation, I'd worn a black tailored suit. My mom had said, "You look like you're going to a funeral. At least wear a blouse with a bow." I'd given in that time.

I'm sure she was already looking in Holt Renfrew for some slinky dress for me to wear to graduation. She was dying to do the mother/daughter grad-shopping ritual, where she sat and watched me try on dresses, and then we went for lunch. Gag me. It was not something I even remotely wanted to do.

Forget about any of that and focus on school.

I got off my bed and went back to my desk. I still had

to go over my physics notes before getting ready for Allie's game tonight. Allie. She'd been upset with me last night for leaving the party. I closed my eyes.

A knot of pain tightened in my chest.

Twenty minutes before game time, I arrived at Podium's gymnasium. The bleachers were jam-packed and the two teams were warming up with layups. I stopped for a second to watch Allie. Sleek and smooth, she looked like a dancer. She had this rhythm to her stride, and when she jumped, she almost appeared to be flying. Long and lean and power-ful, she was definitely the most skilled and talented player on her team. Today her hair was tamed by a purple head-band and she wore an elastic brace on her knee.

I scanned the crowd, looking for a seat, and saw Donald sitting with Carrie and Jax. Right away, Carrie spotted me, waved, and patted the seat beside her. I waved back.

Good, I thought, *Gary isn't with them.* That would have been awkward, seeing as I'd ditched him last night. I made my way toward the bleachers. Partway up, I heard Caroline call my name. I turned and saw her jogging up the bleachers. I waited.

"This should be a good game," she said, huffing a little.

"Yeah, should be really good."

"Are you here alone? You want to sit together?"

"Um . . . I'm sitting with some friends."

"Okay. Cool." She paused for a moment before she smiled, almost coyly, and said, "How was . . . last night?"

I shrugged. "Okay."

She grinned. "I heard you bailed early."

Something bristled inside me. Was she keeping tabs on

my personal life? Why? It had nothing to do with my soccer playing. "Who'd you hear that from?" I snapped. I immediately regretted my tone.

She frowned at me. "Do you always talk to your coaches like that?"

She was right; she was my coach. In all my years playing soccer, I'd never talked back to a coach. "Sorry," I mumbled.

I turned and continued walking up the bleachers. After squeezing by knees, I sat down beside Jax. Right away Carrie leaned over and said, "Hey, Parm. What happened to you last night?"

"I wasn't feeling very well," I lied.

"Ahh, that's too bad, you missed a good time." She said her words so sincerely that I felt obligated to nod in agreement.

"This should be a good game," said Jax.

"Yeah," said Donald. "Allie told me this morning she was going for thirty points."

A sharp jab hit my stomach. He had talked to Allie this morning? I thought she didn't talk to anyone on game day. I had texted her to talk so I could explain why I had left the party so early, but she had said "later."

The excuse that I was sick was kind of valid.

Had Allie talked to Donald or had they just texted?

For the next fifteen minutes the talk was about the party. I listened. Finally the buzzer sounded to start the game and I couldn't have been happier. Wearing her brace, Allie took her position at centre and won the jumpshot, although I noticed that when she landed, she favoured her good knee.

The play went up and down the court, and by the end of the first quarter, the score was 18–6 for Podium.

"Ten for Allie already," said Donald. He clapped his hands, then gave two thumbs-up. "That's my girl!"

That's my girl? What was with that?

At halftime Carrie had to go to the washroom so I went with her.

"Allie's knee looks sore," I said to her as we walked around the court.

"Yeah, I noticed she was almost limping," said Carrie. "I'm really worried about her. She won't go get it checked. As in an MRI." Carrie looked directly at me. "You're the one who's going to be a doctor. Try to convince her. She might listen to you."

"I'll do my best. I think she might be worried about the cost."

Carrie nodded. "Yeah, her home life sucks right now. Her parents refuse to pay for the MRI. They don't care about her knee. They only care about their stupid divorce. It so sucks for her."

We walked a few more paces before I blurted, "Is she going out with Donald?"

"They got pretty chummy last night." Carrie smiled and shrugged both shoulders up to her ears. "But I'm not sure." She sort of sang her sentence. "They'd make a great couple. I'd be happy for her."

"I hope she doesn't get hurt again," I said quietly.

"Yeah, me too," replied Carrie. "But she does need to move on. Nathan is done." Suddenly she grinned. "Speaking of Nathan, he's right over there." She touched my forearm. "I'll catch up with you later."

Instead of going to the washroom, I popped outside

to get some fresh air. I leaned against the modern stucco wall and looked up at the twinkling stars and the huge full moon that shed an amazing blue light on the grass. And I thought about Allie. Carrie was right — she needed an MRI and she needed it now to get the proper therapy. The school wouldn't pay for something like that and neither would her parents because of their messy divorce. I sucked in a deep breath. I had to help her.

"You okay?" Caroline's voice sounded in the dark.

"Yeah," I replied. Where had she come from?

I heard her footsteps come nearer. "You seem stressed," she said.

Now she was beside me. I didn't look at her.

"Is there anything you want to talk about?" She also leaned against the wall and our shoulders and hips touched. I wanted to move away but didn't. I lifted my leg, placing my heel on the wall, hoping that might break our contact, but it actually made us closer.

"I'm fine. Really."

"You know you can talk to me anytime." She moved closer to me.

"Okay," I said. My word was almost a whisper because my throat had dried up. Physically I liked her body touching mine, but emotionally I knew it was all wrong. "Let's talk about my soccer kick. I want to get more height."

Keep it to soccer and everything will be okay.

We chatted for a few minutes about soccer and Texas, and I thought I heard footsteps approaching but no one appeared. Five minutes passed and I said, "We should head in. The second half will be starting."

.

The bright lights of the school gym made me walk well away from Caroline as we headed to our seats. The teams were back on their benches and Allie had ice on her knee. "Your friend is sure playing well," she said, gesturing with her head toward Allie.

"She's going for thirty tonight."

"Cool." Caroline put her hand on my shoulder and I immediately glanced around to see if anyone was looking at us. "She's a competitor just like you are," continued Caroline. "I like strong competitors."

My throat clogged and I flushed beneath her touch. I kept walking. We hit the bleachers and I said, "Thanks for the tips. I'll see you tomorrow." Then I ran up the bleacher steps.

Carrie looked at me funny when I sat back down. Then she leaned behind Jax and put her hand on my shoulder and said, "Coaching problems?"

"We were just discussing my kick. And our Texas trip." For some reason I felt the need to defend myself.

CHAPTER SIX

On Thursday morning our flight for Texas left at 7:00 a.m. and a Podium van picked me up at 4:30 a.m. My breath swirled in front of my face when I got in the van, and I rubbed my hands together. Since it was so early, no one talked.

At the airport Coach Lori sat Sophia and me together on the plane and that suited me fine. I slept for the first hour, then woke up to see Sophia with her tray table down and her books out.

"What are you working on?" I asked.

She groaned. "Social. So. Boring." She snapped her textbook shut and leaned back. "I just want to play soccer and study what I want to learn. Memorizing all this government stuff is painful. "

"University will be different," I said. "You can take just the courses you want."

"Yeah," she said. She squinted as if she was thinking. "I've been putting a lot of thought into what I want to major in. I would love to be a sports psychologist."

"You'd be good at that," I said. And she would be. Sophia

was always helping the girls on the team, listening to their problems and offering advice. And she did so in a kind, respectful way. That's why she made such a good captain.

She nodded thoughtfully. "I like figuring out people's psyches. Especially athletes. What makes them tick. How they handle stress. How they handle pressure in a game or tournament. Look at golfers and the pressure they face every shot." She paused for a second. "I'd probably have to do an undergrad first and then a master's degree."

"Yeah, for sure," I said. "You're a shoo-in for the National Team, and that kind of experience will give you credibility with the athletes."

She turned to me. "The way you're playing, you're headed toward the National Team too, y'know."

"I hope so," I said.

She held up her hand and I high-fived her. "I've wanted to play in the Olympics since I was a kid," she said. "It's all I ever dreamed about."

"Me too." After a pause I repeated my words. "Me. Too." I leaned back in my seat, rolled my head, and glanced at Sophia. "You know, I've done the math and in four years, with all the great players we have in Canada, the team would be so amazing."

"I know," she agreed. "We could be the best team Canada has ever had. And . . . could be good enough to win a medal. That would be so awesome. Can you imagine? An Olympic gold medal hanging around our necks."

Suddenly I felt a hand on my shoulder. Caroline stood in the aisle. "Goalie meeting when we get there." She gave me a squeeze.

I nodded.

After she left, Sophia said, "I don't know why Podium hired her."

"She was good when she played," I replied. "She's helped me a ton. Technically she knows her stuff. And she has so many National Team connections."

Sophia glanced at me out of the corner of her eye. "Parm," she said quietly, "I think she wants you. And I'm not talking in a good way." She paused for a split second before she said, "It's just my observation."

I closed my eyes for a second. Did she think there was something behind the little touches Caroline gave me and no one else?

"What she wants from you is plain wrong," Sophia went on. "You're an athlete and she's a coach. If you ever need to talk, let me know."

I blew out a sigh, turned my head, and stared out the tiny little airplane window at the big blue sky. If I was honest with myself, I knew Sophia was on to something.

Deep in thought about what Sophia had said, I unlocked room 224 and pushed open the door. Loo-Loo and Hazel were already in the room, unpacking. Their stuff was sprawled on one of the two beds.

"You can have that bed," said Loo-Loo, pointing at the perfectly made bed. "You're the goalie and we won't make you sleep with one of us. Besides, Hazel kicks constantly."

I wasn't going to argue about having a double to myself, so I threw my bag on the bed. When I went into the bathroom to put my shampoo and soap away, I was shocked by how much stuff they had brought — face cream, hair mousse, and all kinds of makeup.

"Jeepers," I said coming out of the small washroom. "You guys could have your own cosmetic counter with all that crap."

Loo-Loo playfully pushed her hair up and jutted out her hip. "I might run into a good-looking guy in the lobby."

I laughed and glanced at the time. "We'd better get to the lobby. Meeting starts in five."

The three of us went downstairs dressed in our Podium track suits. Our first game wasn't until the morning, but Coach Lori had informed us that she wanted us to go for a slow run tonight to keep our muscles alive. Jessie and I didn't have to run as far as the rest of the team, so we were instructed to meet with Caroline while the team finished their jog.

"Parm, you will play first game," said Caroline. The three of us sat in the comfy lobby chairs. "The California team is tough and they have two strikers, numbers 10 and 19, who have incredible accuracy, and number 3 is a left kicker."

"What about midfield?" I asked. "Anyone I should watch for?"

"Number 20. She has a strong boot and she can actually do the bicycle."

"Wow," I said. Not many females could flip like that.

"Now, Jessie," said Caroline turning to her, "you're probably not going to see much playing time but you will see some. If we are up by more than three, you'll go in. And we do play a weaker team in our third game. Chances are you'll start that game."

Jessie nodded like a puppy wagging its tail. Young and inexperienced, she longed for any scrap of attention from Caroline.

Caroline spotted Coach Lori in the lobby, waiting for the team to get back, so she excused herself and left our meeting. I reclined in the plush chair and Sophia's words flooded my brain. Caroline had just been totally professional.

She was wrong. I was wrong. We had to be.

After a team meal of lasagna, we all headed to our rooms. Hazel and Loo-Loo crawled under the covers and I stretched out in my bed. "I can switch off tomorrow night," I said.

"Ah, it's okay," said Loo-Loo. "We're used to this. Sometimes after a night out, I have four girls sleeping in my bed."

I glanced over at the two of them, snuggled and cozy under the comforter, and thought about being with Allie in a bed after a night out. We'd never had a sleepover even though we were good friends. A tingling sensation in my lower half made my breath catch. My throat dried and I rolled over on my side so my back was to them.

After my conversation with Sophia on the plane, I wondered if she knew that I was into girls. I didn't want anyone at Podium to find out, but it was something I had known about myself for years. There was a time and place to come out and it wasn't at Podium. At university, though, I could melt into a crowd and be more anonymous.

I put my hand between my legs to stop the sensations.

I woke up dreaming of Allie. We were lying on a beach, and the sun was hot, and we were in our bathing suits. Her beautiful body was stretched out beside me and I was rubbing suntan lotion on her. I quickly sat up, then realized I was in a hotel room. Hazel and Loo-Loo were still asleep on the bed beside me. I held my hand to my chest to allow my heart rate to come down. It was just a dream. The clock radio on the nightstand read 6:30 a.m., and although we didn't have to be up until 7:00, I got up anyway and tiptoed to the bathroom, where I washed my face with cold water.

Focus, Parmita, focus.

When the whistle blew to start the game, I was in my net, warmed up and ready to play. I memorized each player on the field and ran everything I had learned over the years through my mind. It was important to win this first game, and we'd never played against such a tough, skilled team before. Sophia had won the toss, so she sent the ball back. Loo-Loo handled the pass, took a few strides, then did a cross-field pass to Anna, a striker on our team with a left boot and long legs. Like a burst of wind, Anna took off down the field but was stopped by the opposing mid-fielder, number 20. Caroline had prepped me well, because number 20 booted the ball and hard. Squinting into the sun, I kept my eye on the ball and watched it soar through the air, trying to gage where it would land.

"At you, Hazel!" I yelled.

Sure enough the ball landed on Hazel's side and she sped toward it. The ball took a big bounce and Hazel jumped to stop it, letting it hit her legs and roll in front of her. In less than a second she booted it and sent it down the field. I exhaled and jumped on the spot to stay loose and warm, always keeping my eye on the ball. Although Hazel had made a fantastic boot, my midfield struggled to keep control. The ball bounced for a few seconds around centre field before one of their strikers booted it to another striker on the far left.

The play reversed and was once more coming toward me. Our opponents were playing a 4-3-3 system and all three of their strikers were as fast as our Anna. I crouched low, so I could use my legs for strength.

And I watched the ball.

Hazel moved in to thwart a pass, but their striker managed to read her actions and made a back pass. Without hesitation or any fancy footwork, she passed the ball over to another striker, who also immediately passed off. They were quick, sharp, and accurate. Now the ball was coming down the opposing wing.

I assessed the angle. The striker wound up for a kick. The ball flew to the right corner of my net. I dove, catching the ball and holding it tight to my stomach. Then I landed, rolled, and sprung up to boot the ball as far as I could down the field. My team took off running and I breathed out.

The play continued up and down, and we kept up with them. By the half, I had made at least ten good saves and the score was 0–0. We gathered on our side of the field.

"Keep the pressure on," said Coach Lori. "They are strong attackers." She glanced my way. "Good keeping, Parm. Keep talking to your defence."

The second half started and they had possession and used it to their advantage. All their strikers were skilled with their feet and passed back and forth with precision as they approached my crease. So much so I almost felt as if my head was on a swivel and I was watching a ping-pong game. The ball moved side to side as if our defenders weren't even on the field. Then Hazel slid in to try to create a turnover. She managed to get a foot on the ball, but it flew sideways, and in a stroke of bad luck, she created a breakaway.

Focus, Parmita, focus.

I kept my trained eyes on the ball and knew the striker wasn't one of their best. Could I beat her? I stepped forward and out of my net a bit. Just a little though. I had to be prepared to go or stay. She moved forward with the ball, but it was definitely running on her and she was having a hard time keeping it under control.

"Hazel." I yelled at her without taking my eye off the ball. From that one word, Hazel would know exactly what I was going to do if the opportunity arose.

And it did. The striker was running so fast that she pushed the ball just a little too hard and it took off in front of her. In a split second I rushed out of my net and raced toward the loose ball. I could hear the striker's feet pounding the ground; we were in a race. If she beat me to the ball, she would have an open net to shoot into. I sped to the ball, and when my foot hit it, I booted it in Hazel's direction. Ready to react, Hazel did her part by stopping the ball and immediately booting it clear down the field.

I heard the cheers from the sidelines and I exhaled and

tried to catch my breath. The play stayed in the far end long enough for my heart rate to return to normal.

The game ended in a 0–0 tie, which gave us a point.

Caroline greeted me with a hug when I came off the field. "Great game," she said.

I accepted the hug, then drew back from her. "Thanks," I said, taking off my gloves.

She patted my bum. "Get showered. Team meal in an hour."

Our next game was at four in the afternoon, so I was back in my net after a short rest at the hotel. The team we were playing from Ontario wasn't quite as skilled as the morning team, and we took the game 2–0. Exhausted but exhilarated, we were told to meet in the restaurant after we'd showered. Hazel and Loo-Loo got first dibs on the shower, which was fine by me because I had a few bruises I needed to ice. I sat on my bed in my underwear and placed the ice pack on my hip. I had landed on exactly the same spot and it was inflamed again.

Dressed in only her bra and underwear, Hazel sat cross-legged on the other bed, reading a magazine. She glanced at me, grimaced, and said, "Nasty."

I shrugged. "Part of the job."

"Better you than me." She flipped a page. "I hope we can win tomorrow morning." She flipped another page, obviously just looking at the pictures. "I think we're playing another tough team in the a.m. and a crappy team in the afternoon. A good win with tons of goals might put us in the gold medal game. That California team only won by a goal this aft." She threw the magazine on the floor.

"Yeah," I said. "I think Jessie is playing tomorrow afternoon."

"That's good," replied Hazel. "She can use the experience."

Loo-Loo stepped out of the bathroom with one towel wrapped around her head and one around her body. "Who's on deck?"

"Go ahead," I said to Hazel.

Hazel and Loo-Loo were almost ready to head downstairs by the time I got myself in the shower. I told them I'd be along shortly. I had just stepped into the shower when I heard the door shut. Tournaments were fun but you never had a moment to yourself. It felt good to be alone in the hotel room. I coated my hair with conditioner and sang as I scrubbed. What a great day!

I had the towel wrapped around my head when I heard a knock on the door. Had the girls forgotten something? Their key, perhaps? I draped a towel around my body and opened the bathroom door, letting the steam escape.

"Who is it?" I asked.

"Caroline."

My throat dried. I didn't want to open the door dressed only in a towel, but I couldn't really leave her standing outside my door. She was my coach. Why did I think I needed to put clothes on with her? As soccer players, we dressed and undressed in front of each other all the time, so she would think I was weird if I told her I had to dress first.

I opened the door. "What's up?"

"How's the hip? I didn't see you after the game and I just ran into Hazel and she said you were icing it."

"It's fine."

She pushed on the door and walked into the room. "Let me have a look."

I shrugged. "It's okay, really."

She lifted my towel anyway, her fingers touching my bare skin, and my pulse suddenly quickened. I immediately pressed my hand on the towel to keep from baring my private parts. Tenderly she touched my hip, massaging it with her fingertips. "Looks sore," she murmured.

My throat was dry and my face scorched with heat. "It's fine, really," I said backing up so far that I bumped into the wall.

She stepped toward me and pressed her body against mine. "Did you like that?" she whispered, her breath hot on my face.

"Like what?" My words came out in a hoarse whisper.

"How I touched you?" Warm air circulated around my face, cocooning me in some strange bubble.

"This is wrong." I turned my head away from her.

"No, it's not." She put her finger under my chin and turned my face back toward her face. "I know you're feeling what I am."

I looked into her eyes. "You're my coach."

She touched my face. "We don't have to tell anyone. This can be our secret. Anyway, I'm only a few years older than you. I find you so incredibly attractive that I dream about you every night. And I can help you make the National Team."

I shook my head, hoping to get away from her. "I don't want to do this."

She ran the pad of her fingertip around my cheek. Then she put her hand under my towel and stroked the top of my thighs, moving dangerously close to that place between my legs. I quivered at her touch.

"Don't be afraid," she whispered in my ear. "You are who you are and nothing can change that. I bet you're still a virgin. I can change that."

"This is just *plain wrong*," I said, using Sophia's words.

"No, it's not." She brushed her lips against my cheek. "I'm here to help you. Release you."

"I . . . I think we should keep the help to the field." My words hardly made it out of my mouth before she placed her lips on mine. I drew in a sharp breath and although I wanted to push her away, I didn't, because the pleasure that spread through me was overpowering. I knew I was into girls but . . . I'd never kissed a girl and I never dreamed it would feel like this.

Finally she pulled away from me. She gently put her finger on my upper lip. "I know you enjoyed it. Remember, this has to be our secret. I'll get you a National Team tryout, I promise." She blew me a kiss and left the room.

I slid down the wall and crumpled into a ball on the floor, my body trembling.

CHAPTER SEVEN

I walked to dinner in a daze. I felt sick, really sick, because having a relationship with a coach was wrong. When I entered the little side room the restaurant had provided for our team, it seemed as if everyone stared at me. Did they know? Could they tell? What would they say if they knew? Would they think I was trying to get a spot on the National Team by doing something like this?

I hung my head and glanced through my hair to look for an empty seat. Right away I saw Caroline sitting at the end of the table so I immediately took a seat on the other end, well away from her.

"You really stopped that one breakaway," said Sophia when I sat down beside her. She sounded normal.

I just nodded. I was afraid to speak in case my voice gave me away. The room seemed to spin and twirl. I didn't know where to look.

"It was such a risky move," continued Sophia. "You got a lot of guts, girl."

"Thanks," I muttered, my head still down, my wet hair falling in front of my face.

The conversation at the table continued and I remained quiet. My meal came and I played with my spaghetti, spinning it around my fork as if I wanted to eat when all I wanted to do was throw up. Even the garlic bread had no appeal. If only I could excuse myself, but that would draw more attention. I ate as much as I could, which was hardly anything. Finally everyone scraped back their chairs to leave and I rushed to Hazel's side.

"You heading up?" I asked her.

"Yeah. I'm pooped."

"I'll walk with you," I said.

I avoided eye contact with Caroline when I left the restaurant, and once I was secure in the hotel room, I crawled under the covers and tried to sleep.

But I couldn't sleep. All night I kept waking up to stare at the clock radio and think about what had happened. I didn't push her away, didn't tell her to stop. I rolled over and stared at the wall. It was wrong.

So horribly wrong.

It was just a kiss. No big deal . . .

I should tell Coach Lori, but then she would know I was a lesbian. What if the rest of the team found out? I wasn't ready for that. Maybe it would all blow over and be a one-time thing.

Besides, what if Caroline said that nothing happened and I was making it up? Then I would look like an idiot and I would never, ever make the National Team. She would ruin me, of that I was sure. My hopes and dreams would fade in one moment.

My parents would be called and told too. And I wanted to tell them properly.

My billet family would find out too. And my friends.

Then an awful thought hit me in the stomach and I curled into a ball. What would Allie think? Allie. I imagined touching her. I wanted to touch her like Caroline had touched me.

No! Don't think like that.

I tossed and turned all night, and when morning came, I was a wreck.

Focus, Parmita, focus.

When Caroline gave Jessie and me our pre-game talk, I avoided meeting her eyes and instead stared at the toe of my soccer cleat. I did, however, nod at her instructions. Her soccer knowledge made so much sense.

When the whistle blew, I ran to my net and did my pre-game ritual of touching each pole. Then I clapped my hands and stood in the centre of my net. The sun shone high in the beautiful blue sky but . . . it didn't make me feel any better.

My stomach churned.

My head ached.

The ref blew the whistle, and since we had won the toss, Sophia passed the ball to Anna, who ran up her wing. I moved from side to side, trying to stay loose and limber and focused. I could still feel Caroline's fingers on my thighs.

Focus, Parmita, focus.

The ball took a funny bounce and was picked up by our opposition. A warm wind blew and I tried to assess its strength and direction as I continued to watch the ball. The opposition was coming toward me. They were playing a 4-4-2 system and I knew they didn't have the same skilled and fast offence yesterday's team had. I kept my eye on the ball and watched it move from team to team with no one really taking possession.

I could feel Caroline's mouth on mine.

Focus, Parmita, focus.

Suddenly their midfielder sent a pass to their striker, who sprinted forward. Hazel quickly ran toward her to cut her off. The striker kept running to the outside. Then I heard Caroline yell from the sidelines, "Leftie!"

Why would she yell like that? I could see she was a leftie. I quickly glanced at Caroline, taking my eye off the ball, and in that brief moment the striker took a shot on net. I jumped and totally missed the ball. When I saw it hit the back of my net, I swore under my breath.

Hazel ran back and said, "Don't worry about it."

The next time the ball was in our end, I got ready. I watched, never taking my eye off the ball, but I felt so jittery and out of sorts that when an opposing striker blasted one at me, I mistimed my jump and the ball went off my fingertips. I picked up the ball and threw it out. Again Hazel ran back to me. "You okay?"

"I'm fine."

"We can beat this team."

"I know."

At the half, however, we were down by three. I came off and threw my gloves on the ground. Out of the corner of my eye, I saw Caroline coming toward me.

"You took your eyes off the ball on the first goal. On the second, you weren't ready, and that third one was soft. You could have had it."

I glared at her. "On the first goal, I *knew* she was a leftie. You didn't have to yell from the sidelines."

She frowned. "Doesn't matter *who* yells at you, from *wherever*, you never take your eyes off the ball. It's basic stuff, Parmita."

Shaking my head, I walked away from her and grabbed my water bottle. Then I saw Coach Lori approach Caroline. After a minute or so they both glanced in my direction before they looked at Jessie. I closed my eyes. I knew exactly what was going down.

"Parmita and Jessie!" yelled Coach Lori.

I walked over to see my coaches.

Coach Lori looked at Jessie first. "You're going in net," she said.

Then she turned to me. "Parm, you'll sit."

I didn't speak to anyone during the rest of break, and when the second half started, I tried to shake my anger off, but Caroline had made me furious. I was convinced she'd told Coach Lori to take me out of net.

I paced on the sidelines like a caged animal. Coach Lori had drilled the strikers to shoot, and I watched as we took shot after shot on net. Finally Sophia headed a pass, directing the ball to the far right corner. No matter what, I wanted my team to win, so I clapped and cheered for my teammates.

Although the girls worked their butts off, when the whistle blew to end the game, we had lost 3–2. I hung my head. I had lost the game for my team. There was no way we would make it to the gold medal round now.

Coach Lori gathered us in after we went through the ritual of shaking hands. The hooraying ritual was non-existent after such a loss.

"Good effort, ladies," Lori began. "This is a tough tournament. No, we didn't make it to the gold medal round, but get rested for this afternoon's game because a win will put us in the bronze medal game." Then she looked at me. "Parmita, I'd like to talk to you."

I tried to swallow but a wad of phlegm caught in my throat.

Everyone left and I stayed where I was.

"What happened out there?" Coach Lori asked.

"I don't know."

"It's unlike you to lose focus."

"I'm sorry."

"Is anything going on that I should know about?"

"I didn't sleep well last night," I mumbled. *Tell her. Tell her.*

She gave me a motherly pat on the back. "You'll have a chance to redeem yourself tomorrow if we win this afternoon."

And we did win.

From the sidelines I watched my team score five goals and I watched Jessie make some darn good saves. When the game ended, the score was 5–0. Jessie was all smiles with her first shutout, and after congratulating her, I changed into my street clothes without showering.

I avoided Caroline on the bus back to the hotel room and at our team meal and . . . well, everywhere. As soon as dinner was over, I glued myself to Hazel and Loo-Loo like we were Siamese triplets. The minute I was inside the hotel room and the door thumped shut, I felt my shoulders sag. What if she knocked? Wanted to see me? I would have to see her, or Hazel and Loo-Loo would think something was up. She was my coach. I quickly undressed and got under the covers. Maybe if I faked sleep.

I rolled over so my back was to Hazel and Loo-Loo. "'Night, you two," I said.

For the second night in a row, I tossed and turned and hardly slept. The room took on a background noise of fans humming and bodies breathing.

What was I going to do? *Nothing.* I would do nothing. I would forget it all happened and never let it happen again. Tears pooled behind my eyes and then slowly rolled down my cheeks. I hardly ever cried.

If I said anything, Caroline would somehow play hardball and she had National Team connections. That was my first problem with all this. So I just had to avoid her at all costs. If I stopped anything more from happening, it could be forgotten.

My second problem was that if I said anything, everyone would know I was a lesbian. And I wasn't ready to come out of the closet yet.

I closed my eyes. I had to sleep. I had to focus. Focusing was something I was very good at but also something I obviously had not yet perfected. Today's game had made me realize that. One day I would be a surgeon, and if I let my outside life affect my work, I could possibly kill someone.

Focus, Parmita, focus.

There was no excuse for mediocre play from me.

CHAPTER EIGHT

"Can I touch your bronze medal again?" Ruth asked as we sat watching television on Monday night. It was time for *Glee* again and I promised her I'd watch it.

I smiled. "Sure."

"A bronze means third!" Thomas ran into the family room.

"Yes, it does," I said.

"Are you going to win an Olympic medal one day?" He touched the medal as if it was a treasured toy.

"I sure hope so," I said. "That's my goal."

"Mine is to be on a show like *Glee*," said Ruth. She picked up the remote and turned on the television. "You better leave, Thomas," she said. "*Glee* is not a show you should be watching." She leaned over to me and whispered, "If he leaves, we can watch something else."

Thomas's bottom lip jutted out. "I don't want to leave. I want to sit by Parmita and wear her medal around my neck. Can I, Parmita? Wear it around my neck?"

I patted the sofa and Thomas plopped down beside me. I slung the medal around his neck.

Ruth tossed her wild red hair and said, "If you're going to stay, don't talk."

The show started and I settled back, knowing I was going to sit for an hour. But I didn't mind. The warm bodies of the kids leaning against my shoulders, one on either side, made me feel good. First I glanced at Ruth, then Thomas. They were so sweet, so innocent. What if I never had children? My mother wanted grandchildren and I was her only child. Lots of lesbian couples had children; it could be done. I wondered if it was difficult for the children down the road. My stomach heaved and I put my hand on it to make it stop.

I turned my gaze back to *Glee,* knowing how important it was to Ruth that I watch along with her. A few minutes into the show, I suddenly realized what today's episode was about. "Maybe we should watch something else." I reached for the remote but Ruth held it firmly in her grasp.

"Why is that guy kissing that other guy?" asked Thomas. "Yuck."

"Thomas," said Ruth in her authoritative voice, "that's called being gay."

"What are you children watching?" Mr. Reimer walked into the family room and I glanced at him out of the corner of my eye.

"*Glee,*" said Ruth without taking her eyes off the screen.

Thomas started laughing. "It's a show where two guys kiss." He puckered up his lips and made kissing sounds.

In two strides, Mr. Reimer stood in front of Ruth, blocking her view, and he gently tried to take the remote from her hands. "No, Daddy!" She tried to look around his legs. "This is my favourite show."

"Ruthie, give me the remote."

"Ruth," I said, "why don't we watch something else?"

Mr. Reimer pried the remote from Ruth's fingers and shut the television off. Then he looked from Ruth to Thomas. "What they were doing on that show is wrong in the eyes of the Lord. The Bible says in Leviticus 18 verse 22 that 'You shall not lie with a male as one lies with a female; it is an abomination.'"

"It's just a TV show," Ruth sobbed, her shoulders shaking. "You're so mean."

Mr. Reimer sat down beside Ruth and put his arm around her. "I'm sorry, Ruthie, but it isn't just a TV show. This kind of thing happens in real life. Men cannot be with other men and women cannot be with other women."

Sweat beaded on my forehead, and upper lip and my entire body felt clammy and hot. I stood. "I've got a ton of homework."

"Daddy," cried Ruth, "look what you've done! Now . . . now I can't watch television with Parmita." She hiccuped.

Mr. Reimer glanced at me and gestured with his head that I should leave. "You'll have another night to watch television with Parmita. I know she understands that I need to talk to you."

I quickly left the room and headed to the stairs to go to my room. Halfway down the stairs, I stopped and took a few deep breaths. I felt dizzy. This was another reason I had to keep my secret until university. I loved the Reimers, but they wouldn't understand. I held on to the wall as I made my way to the bottom of the stairs.

Once in my room, I shut the door and fell on my bed, hiding my face in the pillow. Why *did* I want to kiss a girl more than I wanted to kiss a guy? Why had I been born like this? If I had to choose my fate, this wouldn't be it.

For the second time in as many days, tears slid down my cheeks.

The next day at school, in chemistry class, we were surprised with a pop quiz. I glanced down at the multiple choice questions, quickly scanning them. There were only ten. I knew the answers to all but two.

Two? Two was so many out of ten!

Why didn't I know the answers? This Caroline thing was getting to me, taking away my focus. I filled in my answers to the eight I did know, then studied the two I didn't know, evaluating each answer. Logically, I eliminated two of the answers, but to me there were two right ones. I tapped my pencil on the desk, thinking hard, and I was still struggling to find the right answers when the bell rang. I coloured in a C and a B and walked to the front of the room.

After handing in my answer sheet — quite reluctantly too — Allie and I walked out of class together. "What did you put for number eight?" she asked. "I put A."

Without answering her, I stopped to rummage through my backpack for my chemistry textbook. I flipped it open and went right to the index, finding the page where I would find the answer.

After reading for a few seconds, I looked at Allie. "A was right." Damn. I put C for that one.

I shook my head. One wrong meant I'd got only ninety percent on that test. Then I looked up the second question that had stumped me. I'd got it wrong too! I groaned.

"What's wrong?" Allie asked.

"I got two wrong," I said. "Two!"

"It was a quiz and will be worth like .00005 of your final mark. It won't bring *your* mark down."

I shut the chemistry text and put it back in my bag. "I only got eighty percent. That's awful."

"Let's get some lunch," said Allie, slinging her arm through mine. "I'll be lucky if I got sixty percent."

Allie's skin on mine made me quiver, in a nice way, and I tried to make like the test was nothing. We entered the cafeteria and all I wanted to do was put my head on Allie's chest for comfort.

Of course Donald sat at the lunch table and Allie immediately waved. I unlocked our arms and tried to smile. "I think I might go to the library."

"Parm," she moaned, "let it go. Have lunch with us. You're too hard on yourself." Then she bumped my shoulder with hers and whispered, "Anyway, Jonathon might join us." She winked at me.

"Jonathon?" I narrowed my eyes. "Who is Jonathon?"

She gave me her famous arched-eyebrow look. "Gary was a bust. But I think you'll really like Jonathon." She put her hands on my shoulders and I swear electrical currents zapped from her fingertips and through my clothes to ignite my skin. As I looked into her face, at her full lips and velvet skin, my throat dried and my heart raced. I remembered Caroline touching my lip, so softly. I wanted *that* touch from Allie. Not Caroline. My coach. I shook my head.

"Come on, give him a chance," Allie urged, gently pulling my shoulders back and forth. "I want you to be happy."

I lowered my head.

She dropped her hands from my shoulders and my heart slowed down.

"Okay, fair enough," she said, oblivious to my physical reaction to her. "We can just go to the movie in a group. It'll be fun. Anyone who freaks about getting eighty percent on a stupid quiz that means nothing needs to have fun."

"Okay," I said. "I'll agree to a movie." Why I was agreeing to this, I wasn't sure but . . . it almost made me feel normal, if that was possible.

I successfully dodged Caroline all week. I kept all encounters with her extremely businesslike and she kept her hands off me. That is, until Friday night.

"Great practice, ladies," said Coach Lori when we came off the field. "We have an exhibition game set up against the Calgary Dinos for next Saturday afternoon. I think this will be a good game for us, as they have a lot of skilled players. You will be challenged. That will be our last outdoor game until spring. After the game, I'll be dividing you up into two indoor teams and you'll play in the city league. I'll coach one and Caroline has agreed to coach the other." She paused, then said, "I have some wonderful news to share with you."

She looked at Caroline and smiled. "Should I tell them or do you want to?"

Caroline tilted her head shyly, which was so unlike her, because usually she was all toughness. It took me a bit by surprise.

"You can," she replied.

"Caroline has been chosen as the assistant goalie coach for the National Team," Coach Lori said proudly.

The entire team clapped and cheered, and Jessie stuck her fingers in her mouth and whistled. Coach Lori laughed and held up her hand. "Have a good weekend, ladies."

Thinking about this news, I gathered my bag from the ground and slung it over my shoulder. I had just started to walk away when I heard my name. I turned and saw Caroline approaching me.

"I want to talk to you," she said.

I waited for her even though I didn't want to. My teammates filtered past me, chatting and laughing and I heard a few making plans for the evening. Sophia was in a pod with Jessie, and when she saw me with Caroline, she narrowed her eyes but, thankfully, kept moving.

"Congratulations," I said.

"I'm asking for you to be on my indoor team," she said.

"Thanks," I replied, not knowing what else to say.

"That way I can work with you," she continued. "Get you prepared for a National Team tryout in the spring."

"I . . . haven't been asked to any tryout yet."

She winked, put her hand on my shoulder and looked me in the eyes. Her touch felt powerful and I wanted to move away, but I didn't. By now my teammates were halfway across the field, and once again I saw Sophia looking at us, her eyes in a squint.

"Your call will be coming any day now. I made sure that the head coach has you on the tryout roster."

"Wow," I said, shocked. Could this be my big break? "Thanks," I replied. And I meant it. I really *was* thankful to Caroline for doing this for me. I would still have to perform but getting a tryout was huge.

But then she playfully jabbed me in the ribs and said, "You can pay me back later."

I deflated like a balloon that had just been pricked with a needle.

When I got to the showers, most of my teammates were already in their street clothes. I sat down on the bench and leaned my head back. Caroline had continued chatting to me for around five minutes about things I needed to work on before the tryout. She said she would help me because she knew what they would be looking for. My eyes were still closed when I heard a voice beside me.

"What did Caroline want to talk to you about?" Sophia asked.

Caroline had asked me to keep the tryout just between us, so I said, "Things I need to work on. I think she's putting me on her team for the indoor season."

Sophia slipped on her black leather bomber jacket and slung her bag over her shoulder. "Oh. Okay. What are you up to tonight? You want to go for a coffee or a bite to eat?"

"I'm going to a movie with Allie and a few others." I took off my socks and shin pads and threw them into my bag.

My answer made her smile, which seemed odd to me. It was almost as if she was relieved.

"Sure," she said. "Well, have a great day off. See ya Sunday."

I slowly undressed, knowing soon enough I had to go to the movie with Allie and other people I didn't want to go with. If I didn't want to see Allie so much, I wouldn't go. By the time I headed to the shower, the change room was almost empty. Everyone was in a hurry to get out and enjoy the night, especially since we didn't have a practice or a game in the morning.

The water trickling over my body felt fantastic and I started to visualize what I would say to the coach of the National Team when he called. In a way it was nice knowing ahead of time, because I could think of questions to ask instead of being put on the spot. With my head back, rinsing my hair, I heard flip-flops smacking the excess water on the tiled floor. I shook my head to get the water out of my eyes.

"Caroline." I almost choked on the word.

She hung up her towel. "There's no one around but us," she said.

My heart dropped to my toes. I quickly shut off my shower and reached for my towel, suddenly feeling my nakedness. But before I could grab it, she put her hand on my forearm.

"It's okay," she murmured.

"I have to go." I tried to back up but I had nowhere to go.

She pushed a strand of my wet hair off my face. "I thought we could shower together."

"I . . . I don't think that's a good idea."

She moved a step toward me and smiled. "I told you I would find a way for you to pay me back." She almost purred her words. She gently placed her hand on my bare wet stomach. "And you do want a spot on that National Team, don't you?"

"This isn't right," I whispered. "It's just not right."

"Just relax," she said. "Parmita, you owe it to yourself to give this a try. I know you're a virgin at this. One day you will thank me because, believe me, I know how hard it is to come out. I've made it my mission to help girls like you. I think it's important that we have the right to be who we are, to shout our sexuality from the rooftops."

She ran her fingertips over my stomach, inching them upwards until they were under my breasts. Then she had my breast cupped in her hand and she was leaning toward me, placing her lips on mine. I tried again to back away but I couldn't. By now I was up against a wall and her tongue was in my mouth.

I turned my head from her to get away. No longer did her touches on my body feel good. They just felt . . . dirty.

"I said relax," she whispered in my ear.

She took my hands and placed them on her hips. "Touch me like I'm touching you."

She stroked my stomach, then slowly moved her hand further down.

"Please, no."

"Shh." She placed her fingers on my lips. "I just want to

help you. You cooperate and I promise, you are going to blossom. You owe me one."

CHAPTER NINE

In a complete fog, I drove home, clutching the steering wheel like a lifeline. When I pulled up in front of the Reimers' house, I wiped my mouth with my sleeve before I got out of the car. What if they could tell?

They would hate me. I hated myself. What had happened was wrong. So wrong. Caroline was my coach. Yet I hadn't run away from her, because she'd said she would stop my chances of being on the National Team. What kind of person was I? I should have pushed her. Run away as fast as I could. I should have phoned Sophia. Now I was as much to blame as Caroline, because I had just stood there with my back against the wall and let her touch me. Everywhere.

My phone buzzed and my hands shook so much I could hardly answer it, but I managed to press the right button. "Hey, Allie," I said, hoping I sounded okay.

"You still on for a movie tonight?"

"Um . . . I don't know." I willed myself not to cry. I didn't want her asking me what was wrong. I lowered my head and stared at the toes of my shoes, my practical, sensible shoes. I'd always been practical and sensible, a no-fuss girl. Now my life was falling apart in front of me.

"Come on, Parm," Allie urged. "It'll be fun."

I stared down the street, and when one tree blurred into the next, I turned and looked at the Reimers' house. That's when I saw Mr. Reimer through the front window and a huge wad of something got stuck in my throat. I swallowed first before I managed to say, "Okay."

Fortunately Allie didn't seem to notice that anything was wrong, because she continued her steady stream of evening plans and said, "Jonathon said he'd drive all of us. He can pick you up, if you want."

Mr. Reimer turned and glanced through the big picture window, and when he saw me, he gave a big friendly wave. My heart sank and my stomach reeled. I lifted my hand and gave him a little wave back. If he knew the truth about me . . .

"Sure," I mumbled. "He can pick me up."

I kept my promise and let Jonathon pick me up at the Reimers' for the movie. I only did it because I wanted them to see that I was going out with a boy. It made no sense, and yet it made all the sense in the world.

"Where's Allie?" I asked when I looked into his vehicle. I'd expected her to be in the back seat with Donald.

"They're going on their own. It was crazy to drive all over Calgary picking everyone up. We can meet them there."

I nodded but my nerves were racing. Jonathon drove an old beater car that looked like a hand-me-down from his grandfather. I got in the front seat and leaned against the door like gum stuck to paper.

"How's your crew doing?" I asked to make conversation. I knew he was on the rowing team.

"Pretty good. We have a regatta next weekend in Victoria."

"You're in the eight, right?"

"Yeah. Eight and four. How about you? Allie says you have a good soccer team. And that you're a great goalie."

I fiddled with the buttons on my jacket. "Canadian women's soccer is really strong right now and we have quite a few who are vying for a spot on the National Team."

He took his eyes off the road for a moment and looked at me. "You one of them?"

"I hope so." I looked out the side window, and Caroline flashed in my mind. My hands started to sweat and I clenched them together in my lap.

Jonathon and I continued chatting about our sports for the rest of the ride, but I was relieved when we pulled into the parking lot of the movie theatre. I needed fresh air. If only I could say I was sick and go back to the Reimers'. But I'd already used that excuse.

Allie was lined up for popcorn when Jonathon and I walked into the theatre lobby.

"Hey," she said with excitement in her eyes. I wished her mood was infectious and I was open to catching it. She wiggled her eyebrow up and down, leaned into me and whispered, "You have to admit he's hot."

"He's a rower," I said with false enthusiasm I could only hope wasn't transparent. "They're all hot."

Allie closed one eye and wagged her finger at me. "I don't know if I've ever heard you say that about a guy before."

I tried to smile. "There's always a first for everything."

And maybe a few more times, I thought. I still had to get through high school.

Allie ordered her popcorn, then turned to me. "You want anything?"

I held up my hand. "I'm good. I just ate dinner."

Allie took her popcorn and we moved away from the counter. "Let's find the guys," she said.

"Who else is coming?" I asked. "You said there was a group."

She sheepishly ducked her head. "Don't be mad at me, but it's just the four of us."

"So he's my date?" I exclaimed. "Al-lie!"

She hip-checked me. "It's not really a date. It'll be fun."

Oddly, this bit of info about being at the movie with a guy gave me a sort of comfort, like I was normal, a girl who dreamed of prom and dresses and corsages. Tonight for a few hours, I could perhaps allow myself to feel the way other girls did. And even better, at breakfast tomorrow morning, I could tell the Reimers, and later on in the day, I could tell my mother when she phoned for her Saturday chat. Suddenly I shuddered. What if he tried to kiss me?

I rubbed my forehead, because once again the events of earlier, in the shower, invaded my thoughts. Events I wanted to forget.

"Hey," Allie said, putting her arm around me. "You okay?"

I wanted to lean my head on her shoulder and tell her everything, but instead I asked, "What movie we seeing?"

As we walked to our seats, I moved behind Jonathon like an awkward duck. Donald slipped in the row first, Allie followed, then Jonathon stood back to let me go in. At least he was a gentleman and at least I got to sit beside Allie.

Although the movie was a gripping political thriller, I had a hard time concentrating and a few times lost the gist of the story, how the characters fit into the plotline. Caroline absorbed my thoughts. Political thrillers were usually my favourite kind of movie because of the intricate plots, but not tonight. Inside I seethed that she had so much power over me that I couldn't even enjoy a movie because of her.

By the end of the movie, I was so lost that I didn't even want to go for pizza. "I've got so much work to do." I begged off. "I can catch the C-Train home."

Jonathon jiggled his keys in the pouch of his hoodie. "I've got a weight workout at eight a.m., and I don't want a late night either, so I can drive you."

"Are you sure?"

He gave me a loopy grin. "Positive."

Outside the theatre I said good night to Allie and Donald, who almost looked as if they were having a spat, and then Jonathon and I walked toward the car. I stuck my hands in my pockets and made sure I was at least two feet away from him. And again, when I got in the car, I leaned against the door.

I had to admit, though, our conversation was okay. We chatted about the movie — well, he did most of the chatting since I hardly knew what the movie was even about — and other political thrillers we'd seen and liked. The drive was made easier by the fact that we had the same taste in movies. Then the conversation veered to Allie and Donald.

"They didn't seem too happy," I said.

"I've known Donald for years and he *is* a bit of a player."

"A what?"

Jonathon stopped at a red light and glanced at me with this playful grin on his face. "You don't know what a player is?" He paused for a second before he said, "I like that. Let's just say, Donald likes his girls."

I had no response to this piece of information, so I stared straight ahead, waiting for the red light to turn green. When the car was moving again, I was thinking of Allie. Was she in too deep with Donald? Would he break her heart? A part of me wanted that to be true, wanted her to be rid of him.

Suddenly every ounce of energy in my body seemed to drain out of me. Geez, why was everything in my life so complicated? Why did I want something like that for my best friend? What kind of person was I? My head started to pound. I let silence fill the car.

As soon as Jonathon pulled up in front of the house, I had my hand on the door handle. "Thanks." I opened the door and stepped out.

"It was fun," he replied. Before I could hightail it to the house, he asked, "You want to go for coffee some-time?"

I tried to breathe. I had no idea what to say. "Um . . ." was all that came out. He was nice but I didn't want to be alone with him again; it was just too uncomfortable. I turned to face him so I could say no, but he looked so sad. I could see I had hurt his feelings.

"It's okay," he said.

Then for some crazy reason, I blurted out, "Sure."

I woke up the next morning to the sound of my phone alarm pinging. Instead of jumping up like I usually did, I pressed snooze and then just lay in my bed, staring at the ceiling. I didn't want to get up; I didn't want to study. And I honestly didn't want to ever see Caroline again. I felt almost physically ill at the thought of having to see her at practice tomorrow.

Why?

Why was all this happening to me? I had always lived a quiet life, never bothered people, did my school work, played soccer, had few friends and no dramatics, and now . . . I had so many people circling me like vultures. My head pounded and I sat up and reached for a pain reliever in the nightstand.

I downed the pill with no water and flopped back on the bed, squeezing my eyes shut. Nothing seemed right. Caroline was my coach and she'd crossed a line. But by giving in to her, by not stopping her, had I crossed the line too?

I had to tell Caroline no more. Could she stop me from getting a chance on the National Team if I did? I rolled over and curled into a fetal position. She said she would. My body quivered and quaked.

And why had I said yes to coffee with Jonathon?

I didn't want to go out with him again.

My phone buzzed. I rolled over and saw my mom's number.

"Hi," I said.

"Parmita, what's wrong?"

How could she tell something was wrong in one word? "Nothing."

"You sound sad. Are you crying?"

"No. I'm just tired. I went out last night."

"Where did you go?"

The glee in her voice grated me. But I answered anyway and said, "Movie."

"Who did you go with?" She sounded perky and I knew the fifty questions were just around the corner.

"Allie, Donald, and this guy Jonathon."

"That's a different guy than the one you went to the Halloween party with."

I could tell she was pleased I had actually gone out with yet another guy. "He asked me to go for coffee," I said.

"Oh, Parmita, that's so nice." My mom paused. "Are you going to go?"

"Sure."

I had said the same thing to Jonathon last night and now I got why I had: to make my mother happy and to make the Reimers happy, and to show the world I wasn't . . . wasn't who I really was.

It was just to make everyone happy.

Everyone but me.

CHAPTER TEN

Jonathon sent me a text on Sunday morning to see if I wanted to meet for coffee in the afternoon after my practice. I agreed, hoping someone might see us together.

I showed up at practice and only a handful of my teammates were there. Coach Lori and Caroline were in conversation by the sidelines. My heart thudded and I licked my dry lips. I breathed in and out. I had to handle this. I had to pretend as if nothing had happened in the shower.

With my head up, I walked across the field, and instead of heading over to Caroline to get my warm-up routine, I picked a ball out of the mesh bag and headed directly to Sophia.

"Hey, what's up?" She played with a ball in her feet.

"Not much," I said. I also started working with my ball. "It's so hard to believe we have our last game next weekend."

"Yeah, crazy. Indoor should be fun, but it's just not the same."

"True. My net is that much smaller." I tried to laugh.

"What do you think about Caroline —" she moved the ball from foot to foot "— getting the position with the National Team?"

I glanced at Sophia out of the corner of my eye, keeping my ball moving too. Did she know something about Caroline and me? Had she seen us in the shower?

My skin itched. "Technically, she's a great coach."

Sophia furrowed her eyebrows. "She's unethical."

I picked up my ball and tossed it from hand to hand to warm up my fingers. I knew I should ask her why she thought that, but I couldn't open my mouth. What if this conversation was about Caroline and *me?*

Sophia flipped her ball up with her foot and caught it in her hands. "Parmita, I really need your help with something," she said.

"What?" I didn't want to look at her, but I did because of the serious tone of her voice.

She met my gaze directly and said, "It's about Caroline."

"What about me?" Caroline's voice from just a few feet away shocked both of us and we turned to look at her. Somehow she'd come from the other side of the field without us knowing.

Immediately Sophia smiled and playfully punched Caroline on the shoulder. "Never mind. By being nosy, you're going to ruin a good surprise. It's not every day a high school coach becomes a National Team coach." Then she looked at me. "You want to run a quick lap?"

Caroline touched my shoulder. "I'd like you to talk to you, Parmita."

My heart raced and my cheeks burned, but I nodded.

"Well, I need to warm up," said Sophia, "and for me that means a run around the field." She jogged away from us.

Now that I was standing alone with Caroline, I waited for her to say something about last night. Instead she said, "We're going to work on a few new drills today." Her tone was completely professional. "I'd like to explain them to you."

"Sure," I replied, totally relieved.

Practice was not what I'd expected, because Caroline kept up her professional demeanour and didn't touch me again. No pats on the bum and no shoulder squeezes. I did drill after drill, and the sweat dripped off my face and my legs ached in pain. When practice was over, I gathered up my things and glanced around for Sophia, but she was deep in conversation with Coach Lori. I had no desire to talk to Sophia about Caroline anyway, so I decided to leave ASAP and shower back at the Reimers'.

What if Sophia wanted to talk about Caroline and me *in the shower?*

Downstairs in my bedroom, feeling angry with myself for even agreeing to the coffee date, I tried on three different outfits. It was stupid. So stupid. Finally I opted for jeans and a sweater and no makeup and hair pulled back in a ponytail. Just before I left my room, my phone buzzed. When I picked it up, I saw a text from Sophia.

"can we talk?"

I replied. "can't till later, k?"

Her reply was short. "lets meet"

"where?"

"call u in a bit"

I trudged up the stairs. When I walked into the kitchen, Ruth was at the kitchen table with her science book open. Mrs. Reimer stirred something at the stove. Crash and bash sounds came from Thomas's room and I figured he was playing with his hockey players.

Ruth glanced at me, then knitted her eyebrows together until they were almost touching. She asked, "Are you going out with a boy looking like *that?*"

Mrs. Reimer turned. "Ruthie, it's none of your business where Parmita is going or how she's dressed."

Ruth threw her pencil on the table. "I hate science. I'd rather be going out with a boy."

"You're much too young to be even thinking like that," said Mrs. Reimer.

Ruth rolled her eyes and crossed her arms. "Dad says I can't go out with anyone until I'm sixteen and then it *has* to be a boy from the church. Most of them are boring."

The conversation was going downhill quickly so I said, "I've got a few minutes. Can I help you with your science?"

"That would be wonderful." Mrs. Reimer wiped her hands on her apron. "I've tried to help, but I'm just not up to her standards." She smiled.

I sat down beside Ruth. As she picked up her pencil, she leaned toward me and whispered, "You're not even wearing any makeup."

I tapped her forehead with my finger. "Science."

She groaned. I helped Ruth for about ten minutes before I figured I'd better get going or I'd be late. I stood. "I can help you with the rest of this when I get back. I won't be long."

"Thank you so much, Parmita," said Mrs. Reimer. "I must say we're really enjoying having you here. You're like one of the family."

"Thanks," I replied. "You've really welcomed me." I pointed to the red and yellow clock that hung above the sink. "I'd better go."

Jonathon was already sitting at a table by the window when I entered the coffee shop. He immediately got up and came over to me. I looked around at who was in the coffee shop, hoping to see someone I knew, someone who would see me with Jonathon and tell everyone in the entire school. I didn't know a soul.

"What can I get you?" he asked.

"It's okay," I replied. "I have one of those cards and need to use it up."

"No, I insist," he said.

I shrugged. "Okay." I wasn't in any mood to argue.

I ordered a regular green tea, because I knew it was a cheap drink. Once I had it doctored with sugar and a dab of milk, I sat down across from him.

"Did you practice today?" he asked. I was glad he initiated the conversation.

"Yeah." I sipped my tea, knowing I needed to say more than that but not having a clue what.

Sports. Just keep it on sports.

"How about you?" I asked. "Did you row this morning?"

"At the crack of dawn." He leaned back in his chair and I envied his relaxed posture. He didn't look uncomfortable at all.

"Why do you guys have to practice so early?"

"Water is calmer." He sipped his coffee. "I don't mind though because it's so peaceful at that time of the morning. Sometimes the water is like glass and when the oar digs in, the feeling is amazing." He leaned forward now and clasped his hands.

"I get that," I said. And I did. My practices used to be like that. Peaceful. For me, being alone in my net was like Jonathon being on the water. I picked up my drink and took a sip just to do something with my hands. Now my practices were anything but peaceful. Today, even though Caroline had acted very professionally, I had been edgy.

"What's it like being a goalie?" Jonathan asked, taking me out of my thoughts. "I think it would be so nerve-racking."

I found myself smiling. "I like it," I replied. "For me, it's about the focus."

"I talked to Allie," he said, "and she told me you have a game next weekend. I might go with her. She needs some serious cheering up."

Immediately, I stopped laughing and narrowed my eyes. "Why do you say that?"

"You haven't heard?"

I shook my head. "No."

Jonathon grimaced. "She caught Donald cheating on her."

"When?" I sat forward. "With who?" Allie would be devastated.

"It just happened last night," said Jonathon. "Some girl from the synchro team. From all I've heard, Carrie can't stand this girl."

Something pinched me inside and I looked away, because I didn't want Jonathon to see the hurt in my face. Allie was probably with Carrie right now, crying on her shoulder.

"He was never right for her," I stated.

"Donald isn't good for any girl who wants a relationship."

I jiggled my keys. "I should go," I said. "And pop by her place."

"Okay." Jonathon got a puzzled look on his face. "But we just got here."

Because he'd taken the time to meet me, I chatted for another ten minutes about our sports and school and homework and stuff that I could talk about without thinking. The entire time, I was thinking of Allie and how the minute I was free, I would text her and tell her I was on my way.

Finally, I felt I could leave. I texted Allie and she got back to me in less than five seconds to tell me that Carrie was there but going soon. I went back to the counter and bought Allie's special Earl Grey tea latte and also a big molasses cookie and an oatmeal cookie, her favourite treats. As I was walking out, I felt Jonathon's hand on the small of my back. My body stiffened. I continued moving forward and once I was out the door, I quickly moved out of his reach and turned to face him.

"Thanks," I said.

"Say hi to Allie."

"I will," I answered. I gave him an ill-at-ease wave and walked away before he suggested that we have coffee again.

The second I sat in my car, my shoulders sagged and I

realized how tense I had been. Why was I trying so hard to prove to the world I was someone else? To be with a boy did not feel right for me. Not at all. I lowered my head until my forehead hit the steering wheel.

Caroline. This charade of mine was because of her.

I drove to Allie's, and just thinking of seeing her filled me with renewed energy. Relief flooded me when I pulled up in front and saw Carrie opening her car door, leaving. When she saw me, she waved and walked toward my car. I opened the window.

She looked at me through the open window. "I guess you heard."

"Yeah."

"What a jerk." Carrie shook her head.

I wanted to say Allie would be okay and didn't need him, but I said, "I agree."

"I'm glad you're here. I wanted her to go out with me tonight, but she doesn't want to go *anywhere* and she insists I don't give up my plans. You know how she is."

"I don't have anything to do," I said. "The Reimers go to church so I would just be alone anyway."

"Church at night too?"

"Yeah."

Carrie glanced at the big gold watch she always wore. "Gotta go. See ya later."

"Yeah, see ya," I said.

As I watched Carrie walk away, I felt no stirrings inside me. Was I only attracted to girls who were lesbians like me? I wondered about Allie. She was always trying to have a boyfriend but none of them seemed to last.

I got out of my car and, balancing the tea and treats, walked to the front door. Abigail answered before I could knock. She must have been looking out the window.

"She's in her room." Abigail kind of rolled her eyes. "Where she's been all day."

"Thanks," I said. Because I was holding the tea, I tried to take off my shoes with my feet. I was about to put the tea down to straighten the shoes when Abigail heaved a big sigh and bent over to line my shoes up perfectly. Allie's visitors must be annoying Abigail.

When Abigail straightened, she said, "Personally I think she's making way too much out of this. It's a high school crush, for goodness' sake. Wait until she gets out in the real world, then she'll find out what hurt can be." She walked into the living room and I followed. "Maybe the cookie will cheer her up," she said over her shoulder.

I went to Allie's door and said, "It's me." She told me to come in.

"Hey," I said. "I brought you tea and cookies."

Her eyes were puffy and a box of tissues sat beside her on the bed. "You're a doll."

I put the tea and cookies on her night table, then sat on the end of her bed. And just like that, the stress left my shoulders and a calm came over me. I almost felt as if I'd arrived home.

"He wasn't good enough for you, girl," I said.

"It's more than that." Allie picked at the little pieces of lint on her duvet cover.

"What?"

She looked up at me and huge tears began to run down

her face. "I thought I really really liked Donald and I honestly liked being near him ... except when we were getting, um, physically close. It's my fault he went to someone else."

"No, it's not your fault." I wanted to reach over and wipe her tears away, hold her in my arms, and allow her to cry on my shoulder. "That's your choice. And there's no way he should have gone with someone else."

"But don't you see, Parm? If I'd given in a little, we'd still be okay."

I moved closer to her and put my arm around her shoulders. "No. He shouldn't have cared about that."

Allie hiccupped. "I think there's something wrong with me."

What if I just leaned toward her and kissed her? First on the cheek. I could push her hair off her face, wipe away her tears. I swear I could taste the salt of her tears on my tongue. I wanted to hold her in my arms. Touch her the way Caroline had touched me. Only this would be right and not wrong.

Suddenly Allie flopped back on the bed.

My shoulders squared. What was I thinking? What had Caroline done to me? What if I made a move on Allie and she didn't feel the same way about me? She liked boys. Or did she really? I wondered about her not allowing Donald — or Nathan — to get too physically close.

"I'm serious, Parm," said Allie, breaking into my thoughts. "Something is wrong. I just feel so sad all the time."

"You're going through a lot." I patted her good knee. "Have you talked to your parents recently?"

"Yeah. It's all a mess. I don't want to go back." She sat up.

"They don't even have a bedroom for me. My mom has a two-bedroom place and my dad is living in Labrador with some other woman and doesn't want any of us. I hate them for doing this to me while I'm away. My sisters phone me crying every night."

Allie reached for the tea. She took a sip and said, "This tastes awesome. Thanks, Parm."

I opened the cookie bag and pulled out the molasses cookie. "Your fav," I said.

"Split it with me." She broke the cookie in two and offered me the bigger half, as always. Allie took a bite of hers, chewed for a few seconds while staring at me. Finally she asked, "So . . . what's up with you?"

"What do you mean?" I lowered my head so she couldn't see my face. What if she read me? What if she figured out that something had happened between Caroline and me?

"You can talk to me too," she said softly. "Everything doesn't always have to be about me."

Should I?

Could I?

A big part of me wanted to speak, talk about what had happened. Get it out of my *brain*. And not just talk to anyone. Talk to Allie. I hung my head and turned away. Would Allie think less of me though? Deep down I knew she would be angry at Caroline and probably demand that I tell someone at the school.

No one had seen anything. Caroline told me not to go running to anyone saying she'd seduced me. She said she would tell everyone that I had wanted it, had easily given in, and it was mutual. And I hadn't pushed her away. She had power over me. She could ruin my chances with the National Team.

Allie tenderly touched my arm and something inside me stilled.

"Parm," she said. "What's wrong?"

I stared at her long fingers, touching my skin, and just the sight made me want to unload. So I sucked in a deep breath, opened my mouth to speak . . . and Allie's phone buzzed.

Just like that she withdrew her arm and grabbed her phone from the night table. "Oh my gawd, it's Donald. Again. He's called me ten times today."

The moment was gone. I sat up straight and looked at my friend. "Allie, he doesn't deserve you," I said.

She tossed the phone on the bed. "You've got that right, girlfriend." Then she held up her fist and I hit it with mine and she threw her head back and laughed — so I laughed along with her. The ringing sound of her voice made me feel better, lighter. There was no way I could say anything now and bring her down. I liked it when she was happy, because she made me happier. Anyway, she was going through so much and was too fragile. I needed to be strong for her.

I looked Allie directly in the eyes and said, "Forget about him. You have —"

"I'm going to move on." She interrupted me, throwing her arms in the air. Then she reached across the bed and hugged me. "Thank you so much. You're the one who's always able to bring me back to reality. I love ya, girl."

"I love you too," I said, hugging her back and letting my

hand linger on the curve of her back.

Then ... I finished my sentence in my head. *You have me.*

CHAPTER ELEVEN

I left Allie's about an hour later, and the first thing I did when I got in my car was check my phone for messages.

There was one from Sophia.

"we still on?"

I replied. "sure where?"

"Tims on 16th"

"gimme 30"

Dressed in baggy sweats, but still looking like a million, Sophia sat at a table in the back corner of Tim Hortons. As I walked over to her, I felt my nerves fray and sweat bead on my back. I had a funny feeling she didn't want to talk about buying a gift to congratulate Caroline on her National Team position.

She cradled a paper cup in her hands. I didn't want anything, so I immediately went to the table.

"Thanks for meeting with me," she said.

I slid into a seat. "No biggie."

Sophia glanced around before she leaned forward. "I need your help."

"With what?"

She exhaled. "Caroline has got to be stopped." She spoke in a low voice.

My heart raced. "What do you mean?"

"I know she's hitting on Jessie."

"Jessie?" This comment took me by surprise. Had I missed something?

"I saw them together and something was off. Jessie didn't look comfortable. Honestly I don't care about anyone's sexuality." Sophia used her hands to talk. "I like guys. Some girls like girls. Who cares? But a coach should not, and I repeat *should not,* hit on players. It's wrong."

She looked me square in the eye and I so wanted to turn my head but I didn't. The thought of Caroline going after Jessie put a whole new spin on things. If I'd said something earlier, perhaps nothing would have happened to her. Poor Jessie.

Maybe nothing did happen.

"Look," Sophia continued, "Jessie is young and vulnerable. And a backup goalie, I should add, who might do anything for playing time."

I'm sure my face, by now, was totally drained of colour. I could hear Caroline's words bouncing in my brain. *I've made it my mission to help girls like you.*

I cleared my throat. "What do you want to do?" I barely heard my words.

Sophia drummed her polished fingernails on the table. "I didn't see them actually kiss or even do anything that could be considered wrong. It's just . . . something about the way Caroline keeps touching Jessie, and Jessie doesn't look happy about it."

I remained silent.

Sophia stopped drumming her fingers and leaned forward. "You're closer to them because you work together all the time. Keep an eye out and protect Jessie. If you see anything, we need to go to Coach Lori and to the school. I'm captain of this team. If she's hitting on my players, she has to be stopped. But this kind of accusation needs proof."

I'm the proof. But telling would mean I would have to come out. Now. Like in this moment.

"I'll . . . I'll keep an eye out," I said in a low voice. I knew I should say more but my mouth felt stapled shut.

Sophia closed her eyes for a second.

"I shouldn't say this," she said, her voice almost shaking, "because I'm not sure if there is any truth to it at all, but . . . my niece took one of Caroline's camps last year and she brought a friend with her. The girl was only fourteen." Sophia put her fingers to her forehead and rubbed it. Then she shook her head. "This girl said she'd never go back and her mother says she's not the same and has become depressed and withdrawn."

"Parm," she said, "I think Caroline hit on the girl. I feel it in my gut. And I did a ton of research on this, read a gazillion case studies, and the girl is exhibiting all the signs of being sexually abused by someone in a power position."

Fourteen? My heart sank. Caroline wouldn't stoop *that* low.

Or would she?

"I tried to talk to the girl," said Sophia. "You know, just ask some questions, but she clammed right up and started to cry. Something was off. Really off." Sophia blew out a mouthful of air. "If we could find some other proof, I think she'd talk. She's so young. She's probably scared shitless."

And I'm not so young.

And I know who I am.

Something hit me hard in the solar plexus. I sat up in my seat and looked Sophia directly in the eye. I had to say something. I thought of how I had to focus when it was time for a penalty shot. I needed to focus now on what I was going to say.

Focus, Parmita, focus. You can do this.

"Remember how on the plane flying to Texas," I began, "you said if I ever needed to talk, you'd listen, well . . . I've got something to tell you."

"I'm here," she said softly.

She knows.

And she needed me to tell. All the words that I had wanted to say to Allie, but had kept to myself because the timing was off, came spilling out of my mouth. Sophia sat across from me and just kept quiet and let me talk. I told her about the kiss in the hotel room and the shower altercation.

Finally I said, "She told me she would ruin my chances with the National Team if I didn't go along with her." I shook my head. "I'm pathetic."

"No. You're not. She used her powerful position to manipulate you, Parmita. You were a victim."

"But I let her," I replied. "She could say it was mutual."

"It's a serious breach of the athlete–coach relationship," stated Sophia.

"My parents are lawyers," I said. "And what happened

to me is my word against hers. With a good lawyer her side, this case will be thrown out of court. There's no proof."

"Then we'll get proof," she said. "We can do this. Somehow. Some way. We have to stop her."

Tap. Tap. Tap. Sophia's fingernails clicked against the table. Over and over. Suddenly she stopped and looked right at me. "We need a photo. You follow her with Jessie, 'cause I'm sure she's moved on to her now, and we get a photo."

My throat clogged. The thought of someone snapping a photo of *me* naked in the shower, being pushed against the wall, with Caroline's hands all over me, made me want to vomit.

"No," I said. "That would be traumatic for Jessie, too invasive. I agree a photo would work, but let's think of the best way to do this."

Sophia nodded once, firmly. "You're right. We could confront her, but as you said, she would just deny it all — and then *I* would be the one responsible for tearing our team apart." She shook her head. "This is so complicated."

"We're smart," I said. "We can figure something out."

"So . . . you're in, even though everyone's gonna know about this entire situation, and that you're —"

I nodded. "Absolutely."

Silence hung over us.

In my heart of hearts, I couldn't set Jessie up. That would be as wrong as Caroline doing what she did to me.

"How about," I finally said, "I make Caroline come on to me again? And you take a photo of us."

Sophia tilted her head and eyed me thoughtfully. "You're sure?"

"I don't want Jessie involved."

"Okay," said Sophia. "For the record, I think you're pretty damn brave."

I took a deep breath. "Can we keep this between us? Just for now. I have some things I have to deal with before this blows wide open."

Sophia nodded again. "Sure. We almost have to."

"Thanks. I need to talk to my parents."

"You haven't come out to them yet?" Sophia asked, sounding surprised.

I shook my head. "Why would you say that?"

"Parm, it's not rocket science. You are who you are. Big deal. Let the world know. It makes you you."

Was I that transparent?

Could it really be that easy?

"To prepare for Saturday's game against the Dinos, I want to work on jumps," said Caroline at practice on Tuesday. This was our first practice since I'd met with Sophia at Tim Hortons. Coach Lori had given us Monday off to study for midterms. Although I'd tried to study, I'd ended up staring at the ceiling and thinking about how to tell my parents. "I have something to tell you. But you may already know anyway. I'm gay." I wasn't sure if I should use the word gay or lesbian. What if I just came right out with it from the get-go. "Mom, Dad, I'm a lesbian but you probably already knew, right?" I really wanted to tell them face to face. They were coming out here in two weeks. I was sure Sophia and I had at least a couple of weeks before we managed to get anything on Caroline. She was like a cat, patient and sly.

"Parmita." Caroline's voice broke into my thoughts. "Are you listening?"

I nodded.

"I know this Dinos team and they have some powerful kickers who can float the ball high," said Caroline. "That's what I want to practice today."

Without looking at Caroline, I jogged over to the net. Jessie followed me, and once we were in front of the net, I started jumping up and down to warm up and she did the same. Caroline was out of earshot.

"What's going on with you and Caroline?" Jessie asked, her words coming out in rasps because she was in mid-air.

"Five more," I said, breathing hard. I counted out each jump for us, and when we were finished the five, both of us leaned over to catch our breath. Just before this practice, I had tried to flirt with Caroline. Had Jessie noticed? I'd tried to be discreet.

"You're acting weird around her," Jessie continued.

"No, I'm not. I'm just asking her for help. She does know her stuff." Obviously, I sucked at flirting.

Jessie pulled at her ponytail, making the elastic tighter. Was that a nervous gesture? I shook my head.

Parm, she's just fixing her ponytail. I was not cut out to be a spy either.

"Do you want to go first or should I?" I asked.

"You can," she said. "I always learn from watching."

I stood in the middle of the net, clapped my hands

together, bounced on my feet, faced Caroline, and yelled to her, "I'm ready!"

Caroline kicked ball after ball at the net, making me jump and reach and catch or deflect. Then Jessie took a turn. It was amazing how precise Caroline's aim was. She really was good and I did have a lot to learn from her. I cringed inwardly when I thought of how Sophia and I were planning.

After twenty minutes or so, Caroline stopped and jogged toward us. "That was good. Parmita, you need to read and react a little better. Sometimes you deflect when you should stretch a bit more and catch. Those deflections can backfire and go over your head and to the back of the net."

Okay, I knew she was right and I appreciated the comment, so I nodded and tried to hold her gaze. I found I couldn't. Instead I shifted my weight from one foot to the other and stared at the grass, which got browner every day. Winter was approaching.

Caroline turned from me and acknowledged Jessie. "You did a great job on the balls shot to your right. I'd like you to work on moving quicker to the left. And you need to continue to work on your vertical. You have strong legs. Use them." She placed her hand on Jessie's shoulder.

The touch made me flinch. That was how it had started with me. Was she done with me now? And on to Jessie? I couldn't let that happen.

Caroline broke into my thoughts and said, "You guys join Coach Lori. I think she wants to do some defensive drills."

Just as we were about to walk away, Caroline playfully

slapped Jessie on the butt. My heart almost stopped and my mouth went dry.

"So?" said Sophia after practice.

"I'll try harder," I said. "I'm just not a very good flirt. In fact, I really suck at it. But I've seen a lot of touching going on between Jessie and Caroline. It scares the crap out of me."

"Lots of coaches do that, though."

"That's exactly how she started with me," I said.

Caroline's next step would be to confront her somewhere else. There was no way I would let her be alone with Jessie in the shower. No way.

"Keep watching," said Sophia.

"I will. And I'll flirt more. She has to take the bait. She just has to."

CHAPTER TWELVE

Saturday afternoon I showed up early at the university playing field for our last outdoor game, dressed in my soccer gear. I had tried all week to get Caroline to hit on me, but she didn't bite. And I'd tried all week to work up the courage to talk to my parents.

I kept telling myself that I really wanted to wait to talk to them face to face.

Everything was about patience. I had learned that from being a soccer goalie.

I walked across the field, enjoying the serenity of being alone on a big soccer pitch. I glanced up at the sky and drew in a big breath, filling my lungs with mountain air. The day was clear, crisp, and calm, an absolutely perfect fall afternoon for a soccer game. Today was our last outdoor game of the season and soon the ground, this soccer field, would be covered in a duvet of snow.

I dropped my bag and began my warm-up routine, which started with a few laps around the field. On my second lap, I saw Caroline. I kept jogging.

"I've got one more to do," I said, rounding the corner.

"I'll join you," she said.

She fell into step beside me. I moved closer to her. I hated this kind of deceptive behaviour, really hated it. But I did it anyway. Sophia and I had no proof yet, but in a way, I was glad about that because it meant Jessie hadn't been hurt yet. I didn't want her to go through what I had. I turned around and ran backwards and Caroline did the same. When I spun around and faced forward again, she did the same.

Was she biting a bit?

"How are you feeling today?" she asked as we jogged.

"Great," I replied. "You going to Loo-Loo's after?"

Loo-Loo was having a potluck party to celebrate our last outdoor game. I never talked about social events before a game but thought right now might be my only opportunity. And Sophia and I figured a party was a good time to get Caroline. I could try to lure her outside onto the back porch when no one was looking.

"I think so," she said.

"Good," I said. "You should come." I smiled at her.

She eyed me a moment. Then she smiled back.

We finished and I moved away from her, finding a spot on the ground where I could stretch, my heart pounding through my jersey. As I was doing the straddle stretch, I felt her hands on my back, pushing me forward, the pads of her fingers like little needles on my skin.

I let her touch me. "Thanks," I said. "I'm not used to warming up with anyone, but that feels good." I stood and shook out my legs.

She patted my bum. "I want to talk to you and Jessie before the game."

"Sure," I replied before going back to the series of stretches I did before every game.

So she wasn't done with me.

As I stretched, my teammates made their way across the field to our side. Everyone dropped their bags and jogged around the field before they broke off into pairs and began passing the ball back and forth. Sophia made eye contact with me and I gave her a subtle thumbs-up.

Then Jessie and I went to the net.

"Caroline said I can play half the game today," said Jessie.

"She didn't tell me that," I said. "But I think it's a good idea. It's our last outdoor game until spring."

"Yeah, that's what *she* said too. That it's a good idea for me to play."

I squatted down and exploded up. "When did she tell you that?" I asked.

Jessie didn't answer. "I'm going to get some balls," she said, and stopped warming up. "We need to practice shots on net." She turned her back on me and walked toward our side of the field. I watched her as she moved away from me, and I frowned when I noticed the slump in her shoulders. What was wrong with her?

Had Caroline got to her? How? When? I gritted my teeth. I'd been watching them all week. What had I missed?

When Jessie brought the balls back, I took one and started moving it between my feet. "So when did Caroline tell you that you were going to play?" I asked again.

She avoided looking at me and quickly said, "We met for coffee."

I moved the ball faster and faster in my feet. Damn.

Damn. Damn. I should have kept a closer eye on Jessie.

On game days none of us liked idle chit-chat. And Jessie was playing today so I said nothing else to her about Caroline. We passed back and forth, practicing our catching. Then Sophia organized the lines to shoot on us and we took turns in the net.

After ten minutes Coach Lori called us in.

"They're a good team, ladies. Sharp shooters and fast. I want you to play them hard and aggressive. Keep it close and I'll be happy."

We put our hands in the middle and did a big cheer. Sophia patted me on the shoulder the way she did before every game and said, "Go get 'em, girl." Then she leaned over and whispered, "Keep it close, my ass. We're going to kick butt."

I ran to my net, touched each pole, slapped my hands together, and faced front.

Focus, Parmita, focus.

I bounced on my toes, going from side to side. The ball dropped and I watched it bounce and move from foot to foot. Suddenly the play was coming down the field toward me. The Dino strikers were fast, slick fast, and skilled with their feet. They lined up well across the field too. When a striker moved in on Hazel, instead of playing her steady defensive game, Hazel moved forward, obviously thinking she might be able to get to the ball and clear it down the field. But the Dino coming down on her was lightning fast and she kicked around Hazel and raced forward. Hazel turned but not quickly enough.

I quickly assessed the angle of the striker's foot. *Eye on the ball. Eye on the ball.*

Was there another striker in passing range? Would she be quick enough to break through? Was the striker with the ball going to shoot or pass? It was a fifty-fifty chance and I had to pick one and stick with it.

The striker swung her leg back and I guessed she was going to shoot. Her foot connected with the ball and I leaped into the air, remembering what Caroline had taught me this week. I stretched as high as I could because I wanted the ball in my hands, and I didn't want to deflect it. There were too many Dinos in front of my net and one of them could easily head my deflection. I wouldn't have a chance.

The ball hit my hands and I clasped them around the ball and dropped to the ground. As soon as I hit the dirt, I sprung up and kicked the ball far down the field.

Hazel yelled to me, "Great save!"

I gasped for breath as I watched the play go down the field. Sophia ran with the ball, her long legs striding forward. My team passed and moved the ball like pros.

Every time a Dino striker came at me, I could hear Caroline in my head, her coaching techniques, and I listened to her advice. I made save after save. At halftime the score was 1–0 for us and Sophia walked off the field with me.

"Man, are you on fire," she said. "I cannot believe you stopped that two-on-one. Amazing. You're keeping us in the game."

"Thanks," I said. It had been the best half I'd ever played in my life.

On the sidelines I grabbed my water bottle and was

taking a swig when Caroline patted my shoulder. "Excellent playing out there. I'm impressed."

"Thanks," I replied. "I tried to do what you said."

"You did." She smiled at me. "I tell ya, girl, you're National Team material. I hate to take you out of the game though."

"It's okay," I said.

I watched Caroline walk away from me. If I ratted her out like Sophia and I had planned, I might never get the chance to show that I was National Team material. Caroline headed over to Jessie. They talked, then she slapped Jessie on the butt. I swear I saw Jessie flinch at the touch.

What if Caroline *had* scarred a girl as young as fourteen? That couldn't be allowed to happen again. My National Team stuff had to take a back seat.

The second half started and I stood on the sidelines beside Caroline, but only because she'd come over to me. The Dinos had possession and their centre passed it back. Their strikers immediately weaved forward, creating a clever formation. Coach Lori came to stand with us.

"Did you see that play?" she asked Caroline. "I think we could use that one."

"I agree." Caroline nodded without taking her eyes off Jessie in the net. "Come on, Jess," she said to herself, "move out a bit." She crossed her arms and shook her head. "She stands too far back in her net. She's gonna get caught."

Sure enough, when the striker kicked the ball, it went high. Although Jessie jumped, she missed it and it sank to the back of the net.

I moved away from the coaches and closer to Jessie, whose sagging shoulders made it obvious she wasn't handling the goal very well. I cupped my hands and yelled, "It's okay, Jessie!"

Jessie let in another three goals, and when the game was over, the score was 4–2. She came off the field and threw her gloves on the ground. "I totally sucked."

"Hey," I said, "don't worry. They're a good team and can pick their holes."

When she looked at me, her eyes were filled with tears. "Caroline will be so mad at me."

"No, she won't," I said.

Jessie wiped the tears from her eyes with the sleeve of her jersey. "You have no idea what she's really like. You're good. She likes you. If I don't perform on and off the field, I won't ever have a chance to play." Jessie picked up her bag and started running across the field.

As I gathered up my extra clothes and my bag, Jessie's words circled through my mind, over and over, like they were caught on a treadmill and couldn't get off. I had to help her. Sophia's and my plan had to work.

"You're still coming to the potluck, right?" Sophia jolted me out of my thoughts.

"Yeah," I said. "I even made a cake. With Mrs. Reimer's help of course." Some of the other teammates were still in close proximity so I had to act normally.

"Ha ha. I'm bringing buns. You walking to the parking lot?"

"Yup." I zipped on my Podium track jacket, threw my bag over my shoulder, and got into step with Sophia. The sun hovered along the horizon line and the air had a night-time chill. Dusk arrived within seconds in Calgary, and at this time of year, when the sun went down, the cold set in. Any day now, snow would fall. Already I couldn't wait for spring and another outdoor season.

"Caroline's coming to the party," I said in a low voice.

"Good job."

"Be prepared."

"Don't worry." She yanked out her phone. "This shutter-bug is ready for action."

"She's done something to Jessie," I said.

"I don't want to hear that."

We walked in silence for the few moments it took to reach the parking lot. I started doing the usual rummaging around for my phone, patting all my pockets. "I must have left my phone," I said. "Or dropped it."

"You want me to go back with you?" Sophia asked. "It's getting dark."

"Nah, it's okay. It's probably where the bags were. Or maybe someone picked it up."

Retracing my steps, I searched the ground as I walked back to the soccer pitch. The search took all my concentration because the falling darkness made it difficult to see. With my head down, staring at the ground, I was totally surprised when I bumped into someone. I put my hand to my chest in surprise. "Caroline, you scared me," I said.

She held up my phone. "Is this what you're looking for?"

"Yeah, thanks." I tried to take it from her. But she just laughed and playfully put her hand behind her back.

"Come on," I said. "Give it to me." I tried to reach around her to get it, but she twisted and darted behind me. Before I could turn around to face her, she wrapped her arms around my waist and pulled me into her. Her breath warmed my skin. Then she kissed my neck.

Where was Sophia? This was the opportunity we needed.

"Stop," I said. I didn't want her near me if Sophia wasn't around. How could I have ever been turned on by her touching me? Now she repulsed me.

She let go of me and I put out my hand. "Give it to me."

She wrinkled her nose and whispered, "Kiss me. No one will see us."

"Come on, Caroline, just give it to me." I tried to grab it from her.

"You were flirting with me earlier. What gives now?"

This was not what I'd planned. I needed Sophia.

Before I could make any move to walk away, which I was going to do with or without my phone, she leaned forward, clasped her hands behind my head, entangling her fingers in my hair, and pulled me toward her. Although I struggled, I couldn't get out of her grasp.

That's when a flash blinded me, lighting up the night for a brief second. I heard a click, then footsteps running away in the night.

CHAPTER THIRTEEN

"What was that?" Caroline asked, frantically looking around the field.

I could see no one. Good for Sophia. She was a fast runner.

Caroline threw my phone at me and took off running, following Sophia. But the team captain had already disappeared around the corner of the university building. I wondered if she had her car in a good getaway spot. There was a parking lot on the other side of the field. Had she moved her car there?

I also broke into a sprint, going in the opposite direction of Caroline and toward my car. My breath came out in pants and my heart pounded, but I kept running.

My hands shook so much I could hardly get my car door open. I jumped in and immediately phoned Sophia.

"Did you get it?" I could hardly speak.

"Get what?" She didn't even sound out of breath.

"The photo!"

"What are you talking about?"

"It wasn't you?" I started my car.

"Parm, I don't have a clue what you're talking about. I'm at the grocery store picking up those buns for the party."

"You can't be. Caroline tried to kiss me and someone took a photo. I thought it was you."

"Parm, it wasn't me. But . . . we have to find out who it was. This is our proof!"

"Caroline took off after whoever it was," I said.

"Meet me at the party ASAP. Someone has the proof we need, but we have to find out who."

I threw my phone on the seat and tore out of the parking lot. As I drove, my phone vibrated. I picked it up to read the text, but then I saw a cop. The sight of the blue and red lights made me leave my phone alone. And breathe. In and out.

Who the hell had taken that photo?

I hit the brake hard at the next red light, almost crashing into the car in front of me, and my phone slid off the seat and onto the floor. I reached down to get it, and as I struggled in vain to find it, th e car behind me honked. The light had turned green.

I accelerated and drove.

It took me thirty minutes to get to the Reimers' because the traffic was heavy and I never did find my phone. It must have slipped under the passenger seat. How I made it to the Reimers' in one piece, I'm not sure. As soon as I parked, I searched for my phone again. When I found it, I glanced at the list of messages.

There were quite a few. From Sophia, from Hazel, from Allie. Missed calls from the Reimers, my mom. And . . . a missed call from Coach Lori. She never called me on my cell phone.

Next, I checked my email. The photo stared at me. The picture was clear, the flash had worked, and the moment was captured. There I was in an embrace with Caroline for everyone to see. There was no doubt about the photo: we were kissing. Or she was kissing me and I wasn't resisting.

The photo made my head ache. But we had our proof.

Still . . . this was not how our plan was supposed to work. I wasn't expecting the world to see the photo. No. This was supposed to be between Sophia and me and Coach Lori and the school.

Not the whole frickin' world.

Suddenly I thought of my parents. I had yet to come out to them. I had to tell them before they saw the photo.

I quickly searched every social network I belonged to, and there it was, in clear view, on every single one of them. Someone had wasted no time uploading the photo and tagging me. It had gone viral in less than thirty minutes.

Who'd done this?

What difference did it make now?

There was no taking it back. So many people would have seen it already and sent it on that there would be no way to remove it even if I knew who'd done it. In the time it had taken to drive home, the photo was all over the Internet. I closed my eyes. My mother was on one of my sites; I wondered if she'd seen it yet. Of course she had. That was why she'd called.

Was that why the Reimers had called too?

And Coach Lori?

I opened my car door and threw up on the pavement. I wiped my mouth with my sleeve, then walked to the side door of the Reimers' house, my feet feeling like they were caked with mud from playing soccer in the pouring rain. I looked up and wished it would rain and wash everything away, but the stars just shone brightly in a black sky. Just like the photo.

I entered the house and slipped out of my shoes, and that was when I heard them talking. About me.

"We can't have her living with us any longer," Mr. Reimer was saying. "I'm going to phone the billet co-ordinator. This is not the sort of influence we want for Ruthie and Thomas."

"It might not be her fault," replied Mrs. Reimer. "We can't jump to conclusions until we hear the full story."

I closed my eyes. Ruth. Somehow Ruth had received the photo. Had she gone on a social networking site? I knew she had an account her parents didn't know about. I didn't know what to do. Or maybe someone had emailed it to Mr. Reimer. Who would be that cruel?

Tears erupted and spilled down my face. I had to go through the kitchen to get to my room. My phone buzzed. My mother again.

In just my socks, I stepped back outside, sat down on the back porch, and said into my phone, "Hey, Mom." I hardly got my words out.

"Honey, what's going on? Tell me."

Sobs racked my body at the sound of her soothing voice and I couldn't stop them. My world was collapsing around me and I had no idea what to do. Our plan had backfired.

"Is the woman in the photo your coach?" my mom asked quietly.

"Yeah," I said, sniffling. "She's our goalie coach."

"Tell me what happened, honey."

The dam burst and I unloaded, telling my mother everything. Finally at the end of my story, I blurted out, "And to make it all worse, I really *am* a lesbian, Mom." My shoulders shook as I said the word. "This is not how I wanted you to find out. I had planned to talk to you and Dad face to face."

There was silence on the other end of the phone. I pressed my fingers to my forehead preparing myself for her disappointed reaction.

"Parmita," started my mother slowly, "are you sure this isn't just a phase?"

"No, Mom."

"You're absolutely sure?"

"Yes, I'm positive. I *know*."

"Okay." She paused for a moment. "In all honesty, I think I've known this about you since you were little."

"You have?"

"There were lots of signs. I do believe it's something you were born with, so it's not wrong." Her steady tone calmed me.

I dug my toes into the dirt. "But you want me to have a date for graduation," I whispered.

"I've encouraged you to go out with boys, but that's because I wanted you to be sure. And . . . maybe I kept hoping."

"You're ashamed of me?"

"No, sweetie. Being gay is nothing to be ashamed of. It's just not a life I would have chosen for you, because it's not going to be easy."

"What about Daddy? He's going to freak."

"Your father loves you for who you are."

"The Reimers won't understand, Mom."

"I think you may have a point there. I can get a flight tonight from Saskatoon to Calgary."

"No, Mom. Don't come out. I can deal with this."

Silence.

Then I heard my mother sigh. "Okay," she said. "But just so you know, I've already talked to Coach Lori. I'm a lawyer. I had to. This goalie coach of yours has breached her coach–athlete relationship and it's unacceptable."

"I'm going to find out who took the photo," I said, "and make sure it gets into the hands of the right people."

"Okay, honey, but I want you to be prepared for the backlash. You might get teased and ridiculed. And you might have to testify in court. And the prosecution will use your sexuality against you. Coach Lori and the principal of your school are definitely going to the police with this."

I pressed my fingers to my forehead again. I could feel the pain in her voice. Pain for me. "I know," I said. "But it's something I have to do."

"The photo is clear proof and that counts for something." She paused for a moment. "Where will you go tonight? To sleep."

"I don't know. I'll find somewhere."

"Parmita, if you need to get a hotel room tonight, let Daddy and I know. We can book it for you."

We talked a little longer, but then we both knew we had to hang up so I could deal with the mess my life had become. I held my phone in my hand, sucked in a huge breath, and stared up at the stars. They sure weren't winking at me tonight. What to do now?

The back door swung open and Ruth rushed out and threw her arms around me. "I saw your car out front and knew you must be home."

The outdoor light flicked on and Mr. Reimer stood at the doorway. "Parmita," was all he said.

"Hi." I lifted my hand in a little wave.

"Come in the house," he said. "You look cold. We need to have a talk."

I hesitated and Ruth put her hand in mine. "Please, Parmita."

Focus, Parmita, focus.

Deal with it.

Be strong. You've always been strong.

I squeezed her hand. "Okay."

I silently walked up the six steps that led to the Reimers' kitchen. I was immediately hit by the warmth of the room and the smell of something cooking in a big pot on the stove, but my stomach was in no shape to appreciate it. Then I noticed the chocolate cake I had baked for the party sitting on the table, and it was now iced.

"Did you ice my cake for me?" I asked Mrs. Reimer.

She gave me a sad smile. "Yes."

"Have a seat," said Mr. Reimer. Then he told Thomas to leave the kitchen.

"I don't wanna," wailed Thomas.

"Go on now," said Mrs. Reimer. She gestured to Ruth. "You too, Ruthie."

Ruth crossed her arms, jutted out her bottom lip, and said, "No. I'm staying right here with Parmita."

Mr. Reimer glanced from Mrs. Reimer to Ruth then back again. "Maybe it would be good for Ruth to sit in on this talk."

I sat on a kitchen chair and clasped my hands together to stop them from shaking. I must have looked pathetic, still dressed in my soccer stuff, and my face all red and puffy.

Mr. Reimer started the conversation. "We saw the photo, Parmita. Ruth noticed it on some site that she's not supposed to be on. With your phone and everything it can do, I'm sure you've seen the photo too."

I bit my bottom lip and nodded. My leg jiggled underneath the table and all I wanted to do was run. But I stayed glued to my seat.

He twiddled his thumbs. "I'm sure this is not your fault. Did this coach force herself on you?"

I lowered my head and stared at the table. I felt exposed and vulnerable. The situation was so awkward!

"Did she force herself on you?" I saw Mr. Reimer's clasped hands and how he held up his thumbs like a steeple. I stared at them instead of his face and still didn't answer.

He continued talking. "If she did, that's wrong. And she will be fired and charged with sexual harassment."

Finally I spoke. "She did force herself on me, but I have something I need to tell you." My words came out in a low mumble.

Mrs. Reimer placed her hand on my shoulder. "This is not your fault, Parmita."

Ruth sat up straight and in her big-girl voice said, "If it's not Parmita's fault, then she doesn't have to leave and not live with us anymore."

I closed my eyes and tried to think. What to say? How to say it? The room hushed and I could almost feel Ruth's anticipation and her mom's hope, I could hear Mr. Reimer's laboured breathing. I knew what I had to do.

I opened my eyes. First I looked at Ruth and tried to smile; she was such a sweet kid. Then I glanced from Mr. Reimer to Mrs. Reimer before I noted the Bible sitting on the table and the Bible calendar hanging on the wall and the Bible verses, done in needlepoint, framed and also on the wall.

I sucked in a huge breath of air, stood up, and said, "I don't think I can stay. Ruth, I'm, I'm so sorry."

Down in my room, I phoned Sophia.

"Where are you?" she asked.

"Still at the Reimers'. I'm packing my things."

"OMG. Like, seriously packing?"

"Yeah."

"Where are you going?"

"My car maybe." I laughed, but it was a nervous laugh.

"Stay with me for the night. My billets won't mind. You can figure this out in the morning."

I glanced around my room, knowing I wanted to pack everything now. "How's the party?"

"It's not much of a celebration, that's for sure. This has rocked a lot of the girls."

"I don't think I can show up."

"I understand. Although, Parm, everyone is on your side."

"I know. I just don't feel like celebrating anything. I also have . . . someone I need to see."

I packed up all my stuff. Everything. I didn't want to come back again tomorrow. My phone continued to vibrate, but I didn't answer any of the texts or calls. I couldn't. I had to deal with leaving my billet first.

I could hear Ruthie crying in her room as I made trip after trip out to my car. No one said anything to me, although I know Mrs. Reimer wanted to. I could tell by how she looked at me every time I walked through the kitchen with another bag. Finally my car was loaded and the room I had lived in for over a year was empty. I hiked up the stairs one last time and stood in the kitchen. Mr. Reimer was nowhere to be seen, but Mrs. Reimer stood by the stove.

"Thank you," I said. My voice cracked and it was all I could do to hold in another gush of tears.

She faced me. She was crying. "I'm so sorry. You don't have to leave right now."

"It's not your fault. You have your beliefs. I respect that."

She wiped her eyes and turned to look out the kitchen window to the backyard and the play structure. "Sometimes I wonder." She paused before she looked at me again. "What if you were my child?"

I embraced her and she hugged me back, hard. Tears rolled down my cheeks.

"You would find it in your heart to love," I whispered. "I know you would."

She pushed my hair off my face and said, "Yes, I think I would. I'm worried about you, Parmita. Please don't leave right now. We can work this out for a few nights."

"I'll be okay. I have friends to stay with." I touched her cheek and she took my fingers and kissed them.

"Mrs. Reimer," I continued, "you have your beliefs, and I have mine. Neither is right or wrong. But this is your house and I must honour you and your husband's beliefs if I'm under your roof. But I am who I am."

She smiled and picked up the cake. "Here," she said. "This is for your party."

"I'm not going to the party," I said.

"I'd like you to take it anyway," she said. "You can bring the pan back later. I'm always alone during the day."

CHAPTER FOURTEEN

With the cake sitting on my passenger seat, I drove over to Allie's.

When I saw her car out front, I sucked in a big breath. No one else's car was here either — like Carrie's — so that was good.

Abigail opened the door and I immediately tried to figure out if she'd seen the photo. Her face gave nothing away. I lined my shoes up perfectly and went to Allie's room. She was on her bed with her laptop in front of her.

"Hey," I said, standing at her door, afraid to walk into the room.

"Oh my gawd, Parm. I'm so sorry this happened to you. Your coach is one sick puppy."

I nodded. For the millionth time that night, tears slid down my cheeks.

Allie got off her bed and wrapped me in her arms. "I can't believe it happened. She's soooo sick. It must have been awful for you."

"She told me she'd make sure I wouldn't have a chance for the National Team if I didn't . . ."

"That's disgusting."

I shook my head. "I should have run from her. Told someone. Before a photo was taken and shown to the world."

Allie led me to her bed and we sat. "Do you know who took it?"

"Not yet."

"Whoever did take it shouldn't have posted it on-line like that. That's a terrible thing to do. I mean, why wouldn't you just take the damn photo to the right person instead of blasting it everywhere?"

I hung my head.

Allie put her arm around me. "Hey, this isn't your fault."

I looked up at her. "She picked me," I said, "because she knew I was a . . . lesbian." After I said this last word, I stared directly into Allie's eyes.

"Doesn't matter about your sexuality," she said. "What Caroline did was wrong."

"Do you think I'm wrong to be gay?" I asked quietly.

Allie gave me a confused look. "No. Why would I care? It doesn't change the fact that you're a kind and generous person. And a great friend."

"Thanks," I said.

I wondered if the day would come when we could be more than friends.

That night at Sophia's I slept like a baby. When I woke up at nine, Sophia was there with tea and a muffin for me.

"How are you feeling this morning?" she asked.

I sat up and pushed my tangled bed-head hair off my face. "Okay. I feel okay."

She sat at the foot of the single bed I'd slept in. Her billets had an extra bedroom in their house and had welcomed me with open arms.

"What a night," said Sophia. She put up her hand and I gave her a feeble high-five. "You done good," she said. "I know it's not exactly how we planned it, but . . ."

"It's all over but the talking," I replied. "And there'll be a lot of talking to do."

"Yeah, that's for sure. Coach Lori took this to the principal who took it to the police. They are treating it as a sexual abuse case. It's blown wide open now."

"Have the police found out who took the photo yet?"

"Not that *I've* heard. But I'm sure the police or anyone with great computer skills would have tracked it down by now. It's not rocket science. In a way it doesn't really matter to the final outcome. This is the proof we wanted. The posting on-line can't be erased now. It's just that you have to deal with the aftermath."

"I still want to know who took it," I said.

Sophia looked at her watch. "Coach Lori already called and wants us at the school by ten a.m. I think the cops are going to be there to ask questions."

I nodded. "My mom told me I'd probably have to testify against Caroline."

"She'll get charged with sexual assault."

"I wonder if there'll be others to come forward?"

Sophia shook her head. "It's one of those catch questions. You hope others will come forward because you want to nail her. But you hope not because that means there *are* other victims. And if they're very young, it's despicable."

She paused. "Well, it's despicable for any age. I'm really sorry this happened to you."

When we got to Podium, Coach Lori ushered us into the staff room. She informed us that the police were arriving soon and that they had questions they wanted us to answer. I was surprised to see Jessie sitting at the table. I said hi to her and she mumbled a quick hi back, then immediately ducked her head. I sat down beside her and whispered, "We'll get through this."

She shook her head. "I'm not a lesbian."

"It's okay."

"Parmita . . ."

I glanced at her, and as she looked at me, her eyes filled with tears.

"I took the photo," she said, her voice trembling.

I stared at her. "Why?"

"I'm so sorry." She hung her head. "Caroline told me if I kissed her, she would give me more playing time. So I did kiss her. And it worked. I did play half a game last night, but I played horribly. So last night I went to talk to her. I was willing to do more, you know, just to get her to think I was good. Then . . . I saw her kissing you. I thought she'd turned to you because I'd let in so many goals. It was like she'd dumped me. How stupid could I be?"

"It's not stupid. She played us."

"I thought she'd given up on me and gone to you. And you didn't need her because you're good. I kinda flipped out." She shook her head. "I convinced myself that if she had you, she wouldn't play me for the rest of the year. I wanted to hurt both of you."

"You took off running. How did you get away from her?"

"Adrenalin. And I think she tripped or something, because I heard her moan. It helped me get away."

"Why did you post everything on-line? That was mean, Jessie."

Tears ran down Jessie's face. "I'm so sorry. I just wanted to hurt someone like I had been hurt."

I nodded once. Caroline had a lot of power.

"It was just so dumb," continued Jessie, "but I was still stinging from playing so badly. I knew my chances were gone. And I knew if you were gone, I would get your spot. It was so-o-o stupid. And I'm so-o-o sorry."

"It's over now," I said. "She played games with us, Jessie, and she lost."

"It's too bad." Jessie wiped her eyes with the sleeve of her shirt. "She's such a good coach."

"I totally agree. An awesome technical coach."

Jessie clasped her hands together. "I have a friend who saw the photo and she said it happened to her too. Two years ago at a summer camp. She was fifteen. How sad is that? She wants to come forward."

I stared at Jessie. "Are you serious?"

Jessie nodded. "Yeah. Dead serious. My friend said it has haunted her ever since. Caroline made her kiss her in the shower. She touched her when she was naked too."

My throat clogged as I remembered my day in the shower. What if I'd been only fifteen?

Finally I said to Jessie, "You taking the photo and putting

it out there the way you did might actually be a good thing."

Jessie looked at me. "You're amazing, Parm. I thought you would hate me forever."

"What good would that do?"

I stayed silent until the police called my name for questioning. They took me into an unoccupied classroom for what they called routine questions. I managed to explain everything, leaving out no details. Within an hour we were free to go. I felt totally drained of energy. All I wanted to do was sleep.

On the way out Sophia stopped to talk to Coach Lori. I would have preferred to just leave, but since I'd come with Sophia and she was my ride, I stopped too.

"What will happen to Caroline?" Sophia asked.

"I'm not sure," replied Coach Lori.

I stared at the toes of my shoes.

Coach Lori continued, "There's the obvious — she'll be fired from Podium and she'll lose her job with the National Team. And because the police have been brought in, she'll be charged with sexual abuse. But so much will depend on victims' impact statements — who comes forward, how many, what happened. This kind of charge can take years to go to court. She could be looking at a jail sentence years down the road."

"We'll need a team meeting to talk this through," said Sophia.

"Monday," said Coach Lori.

I felt her hand on my arm and I finally looked up.

"Parm, you're a victim in all this."

My breath caught in my throat when she said *victim*. I'd never been a victim. I'd always been strong. A leader. A focused athlete. A student who got straight A's. How had I let this happen?

School on Monday came sooner than I wanted. When I walked in the entrance, my stomach ached and my head pounded and my heart raced. But I held my head high, just as my mother had encouraged me to do. Sophia walked with me.

"Is this a captain duty?" I asked, trying to be lighthearted when really my heart couldn't have been heavier.

"You've saved my butt a few times in games. Like when I got called with the hand ball. I did say I owed you one."

I nodded.

"But that's not the only reason. I'm your friend and it's what friends do." She nudged me with her shoulder. "And you and me, we're going to the Olympics together."

"Thanks," I said.

"Girl, you've been through hell. Come on, let's go meet the masses. I'll beat anyone up who says anything to you."

I laughed and it felt good. "What are we, hockey players now?"

"Ha ha."

When I glanced down the hall and saw my peers at their lockers, getting ready for class, holding books under their arms, I was really grateful to have someone by my side. I turned to Sophia. "I am so glad you're with me."

"Just be yourself. Everyone loves ya."

Yes, there were some glances and some whispers, and I was pretty sure I heard the word "lesbo," but there were lots of kids who said hi and acted as if nothing had happened. Even Jonathon waved and acknowledged me, as did Nathan and Jax and Carrie and even some of the hockey guys, like Aaron.

At the door to my class, I said goodbye to Sophia and told her I'd be just fine. Then I walked into the room and slipped into my seat behind Allie.

She immediately turned. "I was going to meet you at the door," she whispered. "But Sophia said she had it covered."

"Thanks," I whispered back.

"You still staying with her?"

"Yeah. Until the school finds me a new billet. Hey, you want to go for dinner with us tonight? Get out of your billet house?"

"Oh, that would be great. Abigail is making me nuts. She is so anal. And she only feeds me food that tastes like grass."

I put my hand up and we did a high-five. Friends. We were friends. Yes, I had a physical attraction to her, but I would never act on it.

Unless . . . well, unless she initiated it.

ACKNOWLEDGEMENTS

I would like to thank everyone at James Lorimer & Company for supporting the Podium Sports Academy series. I feel extremely lucky for the support I receive with every book, from the editorial, to the cover design, to the promotion when the book is completed. I would also like to thank those who read and critiqued the manuscript, and who provided me with insight into the emotions of my main character. This time I had help from some great Canadian athletes: Jennifer Botterill, Sarah Vaillancourt, and Jayna Hefford. Thank you ladies, your input was amazing. And, of course, as always, I must thank you, my readers!

Forward Pass is Lorna Schultz Nicholson's twelfth novel and the fourth book in her Podium Sports Academy series. Lorna is also the author of seven non-fiction books and two picture books about hockey. Growing up in St. Catharines, Ontario, Lorna played volleyball, basketball, soccer, softball, and hockey, and was also a member of the Canadian National Rowing Team. She attended the University of Victoria, British Columbia, where she obtained a Bachelor of Science degree in Human Performance. From there Lorna worked in recreation centres, health clubs, and as a rowing coach until she turned her attention to writing. Today Lorna works as a full-time writer and does numerous school and library visits throughout the year to talk about her books. She divides her time between Calgary, Alberta, and Penticton, British Columbia, and lives with her husband, Hockey Canada President Bob Nicholson, her son, who plays junior hockey, and various hockey players who billet at their home for several months of the year. She also has two daughters who now live away from home, but thankfully, the two family dogs keep her company while she writes.

"Lorna's books are a great read for kids and their parents. They really help teach the importance of having good values both in hockey and in life."
— Wayne Gretzky

"Podium Sports Academy gives readers a look into the life of a student-athlete. Through Lorna's books, we have an opportunity to develop an appreciation for the commitment and dedication necessary to maintain the delicate balance associated with being a teenager, athlete, and student."
— Ken Weipert, Principal,
National Sport School, Calgary, Alberta

ROOKIE

" I hated this.

I wanted the blindfold off and this to be over. I had a horrible feeling in my stomach. None of this was me. I just wanted to play hockey. *Stay tough,* I told myself. I tried to breathe.

"Let's execute," spat Ramsey. "

Aaron Wong is away from home, a hockey-star-in-the-making at Podium Sports Academy. He's special enough to have earned his place at a top school for teen athletes — but not special enough to avoid the problems of growing up.

Buy the books online at www.lorimer.ca

DON'T MISS THIS BOOK!

VEGAS TRYOUT

> It's Vegas. And Vegas is all about how you look.
>
> "You need to lose at least ten pounds." Coach snapped her book shut. "This had better change by next weigh-in. You're the shortest girl on this team and now you're the heaviest."
>
> Lap after lap, I swam as hard as I could to get my frustration out.
>
> *Suck it up and swim, Carrie.*

LORNA SCHULTZ NICHOLSON

Synchro swimmer Carrie doesn't have the body shape that most athletes in her sport have, so when her coach takes her off the lift and puts her on a special diet, Carrie takes it too far.

Buy the books online at www.lorimer.ca

ONE CYCLE

"Short term is all I want. Maybe just one cycle. I need to get big quick."

"You're sure?" His eyes narrowed.

What was with this guy? Why did Ryan send me here? Did he buy off this guy? He was supposed to help me, not shoot me down.

"Positive."

Lacrosse player Nathan is smaller than the other players, but fast and a good team player. When he starts taking steroids, everything changes and more people than just him get hurt.

Buy the books online at www.lorimer.ca